BILLY BOYD

Bonus Baby

Randy Stertmeyer

Newhouse Creative Group

ImPress Publishing Services

Billy Boyd – Bonus Baby
By Randy Stertmeyer
Cover by Daniel Traynor

ImPress Publishing Services
Orlando, Florida
NewhouseCreativeGroup.com
2024, Randy Stertmeyer

Names: Stertmeyer, Randy | Traynor, Daniel, Cover.
Title: Billy Boyd – Bonus Baby/ by Randy Stertmeyer
Description: Orlando, FL | ImPress Publishing Services. | Summary: Humor filled coming of age, middle class meets upper class, with a totally unexpected ending. ISBN 978-1-945493-75-1 (paperback)

For My Wife Peggy

A Shining Example to All Who Know Her

Prodesse Quam Conspici (To accomplish without being conspicuous) - The Miami University Motto

Part 1

It's not what you look at that matters. It's what you see.

Henry David Thoreau

AUGUST 15, 1963

M y name is Billy Broderick Boyd. I'm twenty-one years-old and the only thing I'm famous for, so far, is throwing a baseball and kicking a football for the Miami University Redskins.

My dad, Daniel Boyd, and my mother, Kayleigh Broderick Boyd are both just two generations removed from County Cork, home of the Blarney Stone, which may explain a lot about my father. So, I guess it is pretty clear that my ancestors were mostly Irish. Though, I might note that I am not a big fan of Notre Dame. They can fight all they want. Knute Rockne and the Gipper aside, I'm not a fan.

And, oh yes, one other minor detail... my mother, in spite of her perfectly beautiful Gaelic name, is kind of Jewish/Irish. Dad likes to call her a "Half-Breed."

Hey this is America... the great melting pot, and my mother sorta got melted into this wonderful four-leaf clover clutching, schemata schlepping American miracle.

While her coming out of the blender didn't make some of my Irish grandparents particularly happy, all it took was for my sexy maternal grandmother, Ruth Shulman, to prance her well rounded Ashkenazi behind (sorry Grams) in front of my grandfather Patrick Broderick's craving eyes one summer day at Coney Island in Brooklyn, and nuptials were not far off.

Gramps Paddy was no saint and more than willing to say a lifetime of Hail Mary's to latch onto Grams Ruthie. And voila! America did it again.

So how did Ruthie Shulman Broderick, a second-generation German Jew, deliver a daughter named Kayleigh Broderick Boyd?

Simple. The Boyd part was easy. Mom married a Boyd (Dad) and she's a Boyd. Also, to appease her new Irish-Catholic roots, Grams Ruthie agreed that her first daughter (my mother) would be named for my grandfather's side of the family. The result was Mom; Kayleigh Broderick, later to become Boyd.

Now I could make it more confusing by continuing to describe the nuances of this 1895 Shulman – Broderick bonding. But suffice it to say that, for me, the best part, beyond simply being born, is that, thanks to this most unlikely late nineteenth century union, I have never been required to go to church on Sunday or to synagogue on Saturday (which, by the way, the Jews call a shul, which is the basis for my grandmother Shulman's maiden name).

At any rate, here I am on this Thursday the fifteenth day of August, 1963, about to begin my senior year at Miami University. This is not to be confused with the larger University of Miami in Coral Gables Florida. Nope, my Miami was the first Miami. Founded in 1809 in the little town of Oxford Ohio, just an hour's drive from my hometown of Cincinnati.

Now I ask myself, why am I doing this? Well, first I look at my parents and grandparents. They live good lives day after day and whenever they look back, it is clear to me that they have lost so much of the details of the lives they are still living. They just wake up each morning, take another bite of the apple, swallow and quickly forget the taste.

I have been told that I could be on a special journey this year. If so, it seems to me that recording the details might prove valuable years from now, as the memories would otherwise fade.

Thus, it struck me last night that it would be a great idea to document the next nine months which I plan to be happily spending on one of the most beautiful college campuses to be found anywhere on the planet... Yahweh willing. Accordingly, I ran up to the College Co-op Book Store this morning and dropped six bits plus tax on the counter for a cherry-red leather-bound journal with the round Miami University crest on the cover. I already stand well equipped with a drawerful of ballpoint pens in my desk in room 214 of Swing Hall.

So... Here goes!

Now given the fact that I plan to spend the next nine months, or so, writing about myself, maybe I should start with a little introductory material. A fact-based preface if you will. Then if the school year goes as I hope, I can write a sterling conclusion next June.

My father has always told me that life is just a long string of accidents and coincidences that, even with a little strategic planning, can either become a thing of beauty or a colossal failure. I'm aiming for the former.

But he was right. My coming to Miami in the fall of 1960 involved a lot of coincidental events and far less strategy than I wish to admit. I might just share more on that subject later. Then again, maybe not.

Now I've already recorded my full name, age and what little fame I have established for myself here at good old MU.

To fill in the blanks, my hair I guess you could call a Mickey Mantle cut and color, while my skin is a bit, *Lou Gehrig;* darker than the dead-salmon-pink of my father and lighter than the ripe-olive hue of my mother.

Speaking of my mother, while being half Jewish, let's not forget that she still has plenty Jameson's and Guinness coursing through her veins. Thus, she has a soft delicate nose. You could say I caught a big break in the proboscis department. Definitely luckier than that new Cincinnati Reds pitcher, Jim Maloney. That son-of-a-buck is packing a couple of extra pounds of schnozzola. But that's his problem... I just want his fastball.

As of this morning I stood exactly six feet-two inches tall. At a mea-ger five-foot-ten, my dad says I got a four-inch bonus for graduating high school on time. I tip the scales at 185 pounds, or just about 84 kilos for any family back in Ballylickey who might someday read these ramblings.

As to my choppers, I have been told they are worthy of a Gleem Toothpaste commercial. Fortunately, they were never embraced by braces, for which I am truly thankful. Dad calls them *Chiclets,* as they are straight and snow-white. I am happy to report that they usually cooperate nicely with the family Brownie Hawkeye, as do my blue eyes (say cheese).

Dimensionally speaking, my pants size includes a thirty-two-inch waste and the same for the inseam. Should I be shopping for a new sport coat, I would head to the *40-long* rack. The Miami athletic department has well documented that my hat size is 7 ¼". My mother is constantly lurking to make sure it doesn't get any bigger.

For now, that should be a good enough description of yours truly, Billy Boyd, for those who might actually give a shit.

AUGUST 17, 1963

S o, I realized after starting this process two days ago that I need to date my entries. Thus, I shall do so.

I have also concluded that a little more background information would be appropriate.

Now I have already identified a little bit about my parents, Danny and Kayleigh, and the fact that I am involved in baseball and football at this crazy beautiful place we call Miami University. But as my American Lit prof, Dr Gilroy, might suggest, I need to fill in the color on some of that.

A major oversight that needs quick correction is that I failed to mention that I have two sisters, Eiles and Mireielle. You probably guessed that those names didn't come from the Jewish side of the family. Eiles is just the Irish way of saying *Elizabeth*, while Mireielle is Irish for *Miracle*, which she was.

OK, OK, relax... I'll explain; or keep filling in the color, if you will.

Eiles is two years younger than me and is both an English major and a cheerleader here at Miami (rah rah fucking rah). My mother nick-named her Liz when she first saw Elizabeth Taylor in National Velvet.

Mireielle is a senior at Cincinnati Woodward High School, the oldest public-school west to the Alleghanies (thank you very much). Liz and I also graduated from that yellow brick education factory.

Mom, long ago, dubbed Mireille as Mir. In either case she gets ask a lot, "How to you spell that?"

Truth of the matter is that she is aptly named. Her survival was a true miracle, having been born almost two months prematurely. She owes her survival to one strong incubator and a great deal of prayer by my paternal grandmother, Siobahn Boyd (a name that is just a four-leaf clover way of saying *Joan*). And if you are wondering, how you pronounce that award winning name, try *Shi-Von* on for size. Who knows why the stupid *B* is in there? All I know is Grams Bahny prayed her Catholic ass off for over two months back in 1946 and claims full credit for my sister's survival. No that is not a miss-spelling. Of course, everybody wants to spell her name *Bonny*. Grams Bahny has spent most of her life fixing that mess. She usually just shrugs and tells the rest of us to deal with it.

At any rate, Mir survived and now is number three academically out of 616 Woodward Bulldog seniors. And while dad and I are only outnumbered in the gender department by a slim three to two margin, I can assure you that we are a much bigger minority at the dinner table. Three bonny gabby lasses, all with more than a smidge of yenta thrown in? Well, Dad and I can't compete whether its Boxty or its Jewish cousin, fried Latkes on the table, the conversation is not going to be about sports.

AUGUST 18, 1963

I guess it was predictable that my good friend and roommate here at Swing Hall, Lenny Trimble, would notice that I had taken up journal writing. Sure enough, my old pal LT, known on the football team as *Chief* (we are the Redskins after all and he is the team Captain), said to me this morning, "So B-3 baby, what's with the fucking journal? You going Hemingway on us?"

I explained what I was up to and he took a long look at my journal. After a lengthy wry smile, his only suggestion was that I should continue to engage with my audience, kinda like Huckleberry Finn or Holden Caldwell. You know, like a narrative in what they call *first person*.

While I don't view myself as a barefoot, corncob smoking, fence painting river rat, or a wandering, confused New York wise ass, I did take LT's point and pointed out that I was already doing exactly that. Thus, even though I doubt that anyone will ever read these ramblings,

I will proceed as if it is likely to become number one on the *New York Times Best Seller List (fat chance).*

Oh, by the way, thanks to LT, most of my friends and teammates call me *B-3*. You see, in high school I was known as "Triple-B" as in Billy Broderick Boyd" (that's three Bs folks). Then when I became a fastball throwing pitcher, LT decided that I (B-3) was throwing BBs, (fast little balls that are hard to hit) and which require a gun to shoot. The segue for him was easy. I also became *Gunner* to many of my teammates. Now, everybody calls me *B-3* or *Gunner*, except my sisters who still insist on *Billy* and my mother, the only person on the planet who calls me *William*. At any rate that gives me more names than a college boy deserves.

LT and I have been best pals since the seventh grade, when we both showed up in the same homeroom at the new Woodward High School in 1954. Within days he went from Lenny Trimble to *LT* while, as I said, I took on the moniker, *B-3*. We've been teammates, roommates and best friends ever since.

And, oh yes, LT did make one more point. He said to me, "B-3, the one thing that makes you interesting is your ninety mile an hour fastball and your fall-off-the-table curveball, which will likely have you pitching in the World Series before you can say *Sandy Koufax*. Don't you think you should explain how you went from a centerfielder to an All-American pitcher?"

LT was two-for-two on my journal exploits this morning.

Now I have to admit that there was a good dose of serendipity in how I wound up pitching (no pun intended) for our beloved Red-skins.

It was a year and a half ago in early April. We were playing our fifth game of the 1962 season against the highly touted Ohio University Bobcats.

We had beaten Xavier in the first game of the season on a triple by our very talented centerfielder (me), thank you very much. But we then lost the next four straight.

I stood out in centerfield in the bottom of fifth inning as we were once again getting our collective asses kicked. Three homeruns had sailed over my head into homer-land just in the inning, and we now trailed OU by the embarrassing score of 12-0.

Our coach, Andy Anderson, was midway through destroying our dugout as balls, bats and batting helmets bounced off of the concrete walls. Red Graf, our fourth pitcher in the game, stood dismayed gazing at the blue sky waiting for Andy to wear himself out. When Coach Woodrow "Andy" Anderson gets really pissed he switches from standard cursing to speaking in tongues.

In centerfield I heard him screaming, "Motar flickcock sumofa basstenero pack of richie."

Finally, our coach collected himself and headed to the mound. At the same time, I was overcome with a strange and overpowering impulse to head to the mound myself. Suddenly, there I stood along with Andy, Red, and Len Billet, our catcher.

Andy was so pissed he didn't notice me at first. Finally, he regained consciousness, spotted me and said forcefully, "Jesus H Christ, Boyd, what the hell are you doing here? I don't need any of your shit. Get back in centerfield where you belong."

I looked Andy straight in the eye and said, "I want to pitch, coach."

Andy said, "Jesus Christ!"

Billet said, "Hell coach, he's got a strong arm. Give him a chance."

Andy said, "Jesus Christ!!"

Red holding out the ball said, "Coach, I just don't have it today."

To that, Andy responded, "Jessssus- K-Rist!!!"

I said again, this time more forcefully, "I want to pitch."

The Homeplate umpire snuck up on or little gathering and yelled, "Play ball!"

That seemed to snap Andy back to reality. He looked at Red and then at me speaking calmly now, "Red, you stink. Go sit down. You're done for the day."

Then turning back to me and smiling like he was a fox who had found his way into the chicken coop, he said, "OK, Boyd, so you want to pitch? Well, it's a cinch none of our pitchers do. What the shit. Go ahead and pitch."

With that he handed me the ball and headed back toward our dugout shouting, "Jimmy Sterling you are now playing centerfield. Get your chickenshit ass out there." (Andy was a great motivator of men).

He then advised the umpire what he was up to. The next thing I know I heard the Ohio U PA announcer's voice blaring from the speakers, "Now playing centerfield and batting ninth for Miami, number 36, Jim Sterling. Now pitching for Miami, number 10, Billy Boyd.

While trying not to shit my pants, I heard Len Billett ask, "Hey Billy, whatdaya throw? I know you have a fastball and I've seen you throw a knuckleball. Can you throw a curve?"

I responded with the truth, "Hell, Lenny, we better stick with the heat."

Len processed that and then insisted, "No. Here's what we're going to do. You throw knuckleballs until I flash you a one. One is fastball and two is knuckleball. And don't worry about where that number 2 pitch goes. We need to put the fear of God in these cockamamie Bobcats. Trust me Billy. OK, you get six warmup pitches. Just nice and easy. Then we throw a couple of knuckleballs to this knucklehead"

Lenny trotted back behind the plate while there I stood realizing I had lost my mind. Of my warmups, Lenny was able to knock down four of them. I heard Andy say, "Jesus Christ, sumamudder sleektop holly pack of fukkin' pack of richie."

Finally, the Ump screamed "Play Ball," and Lenny flashed me a 2.

I went into a convoluted version of a full windup digging my finger tips into the seams of the Rawlings baseball I now nervously held in my right hand. *If Len wanted a knuckleball, I'll give him a knuckleball.*

I let go of the ball way too soon and it sailed wildly over the batter's head.

Len flashed another 2. I threw a great floater. You could count the stiches on that baby. But again, it was way high and inside, further agitating the OU batter, while Andy was close to having a stroke.

Len flashed a 1. The one thing I was sure of was my ability to throw hard. But it headed right at the batter's head. It didn't hit him but it was a close shave (pun intended).

Len smiled at the disjointed batter and said, "Better hang loose, he's not a pitcher and has no idea where the ball is going."

Then my life changed.

The OU batter took two perfect fastballs and then made a very late slap at the third heater. I had my first college career K. For all of you opera fans, that's a strikeout.

Quickly I collected two more Ks on six straight fastballs, and the Miami nine trotted happily off of the field.

To make a long story short, I finished the game without giving up any hits, though I did hit two Bobcats and had four wild pitches. But they hadn't scored another run.

The next morning LT slapped down a copy of the *Hamilton Journal* onto my desk opened to the sports page exhibiting a bold-print headline reading, *Centerfielder, Miami's Best Pitcher?*

As I closely perused the story, it read something like Grantland Rice might have written, describing the Four Horseman at Notre Dame (have I mentioned that I'm not a fan of Notre Dame?).

> *Billy Boyd, Miami's star Centerfielder, may have made the trip of a lifetime yesterday in Athens Ohio when he moseyed the short distance from the dark shadows of the centerfield wall into the bright sunlight of the pitcher's mound. Over the next five innings his performance proved that he has been position a hundred feet, or more, too far from Homeplate.*

Now Hugh Bailey, Sports Editor at the *Journal* is not now, nor will he ever be, Grantland Rice. But as I read his piece, it became clear that I might get to pitch again for the Redskins.

On the bus ride back to Oxford Andy hadn't even acknowledged my rough yet sterling performance.

But Hugh Bailey had. The rest of the season went by quicker than one of my best fastballs. I had thrown two no-hitters and was slowly developing a curveball to go along with my floater and my heat.

Our 1963 season clearly proved that my pitching talent was no fluke. I won all 13 games I started, threw three no-hitters (including one against Notre Dame... take that Rockne), and had the lowest ERA in all of college baseball.

On the June 3 issue of *Sports Illustrated*, the cover graced by a picture of Bob Hope in a Cleveland Indians uniform (he owns a piece of the Indians), and had a snippet about me in their *Faces in the Cro*wd section. I took a lot of shit about that from LT and my sisters. But Dad bought a dozen copies and took my mom to see *Critics Choice* at the Valley Theater, staring Bob Hope.

So, I guess you could say the pitching thing was working out for me. And now I have fulfilled LT's request for telling the story of how I got from centerfield to the pitcher's mound. And we haven't even scratched the surface on my football adventures.

AUGUST 22, 1963

As I have mentioned, in addition to my baseball exploits with our beloved Redskins, I am also the place kicker on our renowned football team. Practice started for us on August 8th. Each morning and afternoon I have practiced points after, field goals and kick-offs while the rest of the squad beat the holly shit out of each other.

Our old coach, Miami legend Johnny Pont, after a great 1962 season which included a trip to the Tangerine Bowl, left for more moolah at Yale. He has been replaced by former Ohio State assistant coach, Bo Schembechler. Now if Ohio State coach Woody Hayes is intense, Schembechler is like Hayes after too much coffee.

Coach Pont, like Woody, had been passionate about the game. After a couple of weeks, we have discovered that Bo was closer to insane. He has worked our asses off. I have never run so many wind sprints. The team has been in full pads since day one and the contact has been intense.

If Andy could have his way, I would be working on my curve ball when not booting a football. But the NCAA sees it differently. Throwing a baseball at football practice could cost me my senior year in baseball. So, my glove has stayed safely stored in the closet at my dorm and Andy has done all he could to lessen any contact I might have on the football field.

One thing for sure is that we will be in great condition for our opener against Xavier on September 27th. How good we might play remains to be seen.

AUGUST 24, 1963

By the way, I haven't mentioned it, but I have a girlfriend. Her name is Nancy Brooks. I call her Nan or Brooksie, depending on my mood. She lives in Lexington, on a horse farm that sometimes seems like a foreign country when compared to my humble middle-class neighborhood of Roselawn in Cincinnati. Over the past eight months I have become fairly familiar with US route 27 that weaves its way from Oxford, through Cincinnati on down to Lexington. I have also spent a small fortune in dimes calling her this past summer.

But what makes the three-hour drives and the rolls of dimes more than worthwhile is that Nan is a mix of "Playboy" centerfold and "Vogue Magazine" material... sexy and sophisticated.

Brooksie and I got together last year after meeting in a Classics Literature class... not just because of her Playboy qualifications, but because she is complexed and very self-assured, which I happen to find to be very sexy.

And she is one smart cookie too, which can be somewhat intimidating at times. I cannot think of anything about her not to like, which, I guess, makes her just about perfect. We got together as a result of my typical impulsive behavior, not unlike how I went from centerfield to the pitcher's mound.

I first gazed upon Nan's magnificence the first week of school last year, when I spotted her at the Student Union, or the Rez, as we like to call it, where she sat at a widow booth with a group of her friends. It's called the Rez which is *Miami-speak* for Reservation, because we are the Miami Redskins after all. But, I digress, as I often do.

Nan was simply stunning; breathtaking; Goddess-like. I could not take my eyes off of her. Then she left and disappeared from my life until she walked back into it the first day of my Classics 201 class last January.

I am not a big believer in fate, but I am really thankful for the coincidence that brought her back into view. So, there we sat three rows apart in Dr. Adamson's one o'clock highly coveted class that would hopefully make us close pals with guys like Moliere, Chaucer, Rabelais, Rousseau, Swift and Goethe to name a few. Frankly, my mother was more excited than I was about me taking this class from the renowned Rhodes Scholar, Frederick Adamson. But my enthusiasm tripled when Brooksie appeared. It was both intimidating and comforting.

There was one major problem however. She looked though me as if I were not there. No matter how hard I tried to make eye contact, nothing... zilch... a big fat zero.

And so it went, throughout January and well into February. My desire to engage with her became more and more intense, while my attention to the Classics ala Adamson continually waned. I proudly carry a 3.8 grade point average. But it was looking like I might be working toward the first C of my college career... not good.

Then one day as the old Prof was waxing on and on about Don Quixote and his silly man-servant Sancho Panza, and I sat mesmerized with Nancy Brooks, fancying myself as her man-servant, Adamson woke me from my stupor.

"Mr. Boyd," I half heard him in the distance. Then more sternly and clearly the second time, "Mr. Boyd, Mr. Boyd!! Would you kindly reward us with your attention?"

Then he continued, "You know Mr. Boyd, I have been told by several faculty members that you have done much on this campus to dispel the myth of the proverbial dumb jock. However, we are almost half way through the semester and I would submit that you have yet to grace this group with the slightest indication that you have any interest in being here. Now may I suggest that you either allow all of us to know what it is on the other side of the room that you find so intriguing, or else, please answer my question."

Well since I hadn't heard the question, I decided my only choice was to go with option A.

Thus, I blurted out the truth.

"It's Nancy Brooks that I find intriguing, Dr. Adamson."

There was a smattering of muffled laughter throughout the room, and a red-faced Nancy Brooks looking at me blushing enough to make her a real Miami Redskin.

Oh boy, this isn't good, I thought.

Adamson clearly confirmed that he concurred when he said, "I'm sure Miss Brooks is very happy to know that you find her intriguing. However, I would really rather know your feelings on whether or not it is Cervantes' ability to relate sixteenth century spirit of protest that makes *Don Quixote* worth our time for consideration in this class. And since you seem to share the same romantic notions as Don

Quixote, may I request that you rise and address your answer directly to Miss Brooks."

Oh shit, I thought. *This really is not good*. I could tell Adamson was not joking around. So, I slowly stood up and turned toward Nan without making eye contact and let her rip with an answer that went something like this.

"Yes, sir. Well, in my opinion the greatness of Don Quixote lies in more positive virtues than are found in the spirit of protest, however practical and worthwhile that spirit may be. I think that the real greatness lies in the comprehensive view of sixteenth century Spain, in the breath and depth of its humanity and in the stature of its central character."

Feeling a bit more relaxed I continued, "Don Quixote de la Mancha, for all of his absurdities, is essentially right, just as his squire Sancho Panza is right. The generosity, courage and idealism of Don Quixote, as crazy as it may seem, are complimentary to the realism of Sancho. The virtue of both characters seems to meld together and are essential to the whole man."

Now on a roll I concluded by saying, "The thing that I think Cervantes makes clear is that the business of humanity in this world is largely furthered by both sun-dazzled nobility and earth-bound commonplace, however absurd either one at times may seem to be. That was true four hundred years ago and remains true today."

Those were not my exact words, but it's close. After wiping the beads of sweat from my forehead I turned back toward my teacher and slowly sat back down.

With that, Adamson displaying a wry smile quietly said, "Touché Mr. Boyd. Thank you for that. I assume that I have regained your attention?"

"Yes sir," I lied. And the minute Adamson turned his focus back to the subject matter I snuck a quick peak at Nan. To my great surprise, she was looking right at me with a shy but genuine smile.

When the bell ending our class finally rang, I bolted from my desk only to see Nan rush out the door. But when I exited the room, I found her waiting for me.

I tried to explain, "Listen Nancy, I'm really sorry. I don't know why I said that. Please forgive me. I..."

At that point she put her hand to my lips and said forcefully, "I want to talk to you but I can't right now. I have a two o'clock class. Can you meet me at Tuffy's at three?"

Well, let me tell ya, she didn't have to ask twice and I mumbled, "Sure. Three o'clock. Fine."

With that she spun away from me and disappeared into the crowd of students now passing through the second floor of Upham Hall.

As I scurried back to my room at Swing Hall, it hit me that what lie ahead was problematic on a few fronts.

First, I had a fairly serious girlfriend already. Toni Jansen and I had been locked in place for more than a year. Second, Toni was my sister Liz' good friend, roommate and fellow cheerleader. And third, I had to admit that for some reason I felt considerably inferior to Nancy Brooks.

I continued to mull all of that over until I burst through the door of my room, where I found my best friend and roommate, LT, taking his mid-day snore.

After bringing LT up to date, he said to me, "Well, fuck me to tears B3. You be staring at a genuine jackpot. I wouldn't want to be in your penny loafers."

I looked down at my feet to discover LT had nailed that one. I was, indeed, wearing my brown Bass Weejuns, sans pennies.

We were having an early Spring day. So, before heading to Tuffy's I discarded my blue Pea-Jacket and replaced it with my red Miami Letter sweater… sis-boom-ba!!

Tuffy's was across the street from Swing Hall and I arrived a little before three. As always, after negotiating the three steps down to the entrance and pushing through the heavy glass door into Tuffy's, I took a quick glance to the left above the soda fountain to be sure the publicity photo of me was hanging straight. Pathetic, I know… but we all have egos. I took my favorite booth by a window looking out onto Withrow Street.

I dropped a nickel in the jukebox hanging securely on the wall beneath the window and hit B-6. Immediately, Lenny Welch rewarded my five cents with his current rendition of "Scotch and Soda".

From the first day I walked into Tuffy's I have been fascinated with the tables and their carved messages that stands as a permanent record of young love at Miami over several decades, carefully protected by regular coats of lacquer that gives them a thick glass-like sheen.

As I ran my fingertips over PT + AG - 1953, Bob loves Susan '48, and Tom loves all Thetas – '59, Nancy snuck up on me, softly touching my shoulder from behind. I looked up and was, once again, struck by her overwhelming beauty.

Now, I have to admit I have been fortunate when it comes to pretty girls. Toni is very attractive in an *All-American Girl* kind of way. But Nan has the breath-taking beauty of a Kim Novak, or a Rita Hayworth, with the sweetness of a Grace Kelly or a Natalie Wood. In other words, unattainable.

"Hi," she said as she slid into the seat across from me.

She had obviously noticed me casing out the table top and commented, "I love to study these tables too. Some of them were etched way back in the Thirties. Can you imagine this place back then?"

I began to apologize again, but Nan stopped me.

Reaching across the table, she took my hand in hers and said, "Please don't apologize. It was embarrassing at first, but it turned out to be one of the sweetest things that has ever happened to me. And you were fabulous. Adamson was trying to make you look foolish. Your answer was brilliant. You threw it right back at him and he knew it."

I realized that she still held on to my hand as I tried to digest just what was going on.

The next thing I knew, I squeezed her hand and blurted out, "You have the most beautiful eyes."

Using those same baby-blues, she looked me dead in the eye and said, "Are you in love with that Toni what's her name?"

Impulsively I let a laugh. How the hell did she know about Toni and me?

I managed to mumble a feeble answer. "Hell Nancy, I'm not sure I even know what love is. Toni is my sister's roommate and we have been dating since she showed up on campus. I certainly care for her."

"Then why did you say what you said in class today?" she asked.

I didn't have an answer for that beaut of a question. So, I just sat there in silence, the Kingston Trio now filling the void over the abundant speakers in Tuffy's.

Nan released my hand, the gleam gone from her expression. She selected her response carefully. Finally, she said almost in a whisper, "Billy, I am pretty sure I want to be with you."

Clearly struggling, she continued, "Oh, this is so embarrassing. There are things I want to say to you, but I'm afraid they will sound terribly foolish."

I reached back across the table and again took her hand in mine. Giving it another squeeze, I assured her that her thoughts could safely be shared with me.

Over the next hour Nan and I quickly worked through the process of getting to know each other as she sipped on a cherry coke while I devoured three nectar phosphates and every word she had to say.

By 4:30 it had become clear to both of us that we had much in common, including a love for sports, music, politics, movies, and books. The one thing she didn't share was that she had an outrageously rich father. But at that moment that would have just seemed like background noise.

We also had decided that we should have our first date the following evening. I asked her to go with me to see "The Days of Wine and Roses" at the Western Theater uptown on High Street. She must have liked Jack Lemon and Lee Remick because she accepted. Or maybe it was the Andy Williams version of the theme song that seemed to be playing on WSAI radio every 10 minutes.

All I can say is that the date went very well. On the other hand, explaining this to Toni... well that's another story for another day. It's time I get some Zs. More to follow. Good night one and all.

AUGUST 25, 1963

G reetings and salutations, sports fans (as Professor Jellison says
at the start of each Diplomatic History class). I gave the old
journal the weekend off. Wish I could say that Coach Bo had done
the same for us Redskins. But no such luck.

We had our first full pads scrimmage on Saturday. I had four field
goals which really pissed Bo off. If I'm putting up 3s then our offense
isn't putting up 6s. On the other-hand our D is looking strong. The
Red squad beat the White squad, meaning our first team beat our
second team... but let's face it... that's why they're the first team.

The big development over the weekend is that my sister Liz informed me that she is headed to Washington DC with my mother,
my sister Mir and my old girlfriend Toni Jansen. Which reminds me
I still haven't mentioned how my breakup with Toni went. The short
version is that, as the new saying goes, I screwed the pooch.

But first back to why the ladies in my family are boarding a chartered train tomorrow at the Cincinnati Union Terminal that is headed to DC. On Wednesday, there is going to be this big deal they are calling *The March on Washington for Jobs and Freedom*, which is hoping to draw over 100,000 people. The purpose is to focus on civil rights and employment for American Negroes. God knows if there is one thing that needs attention in this country, it is how we treat our Negro citizens. And if you want an education on that subject just ask my mother and then brace yourself for the answer.

Dad's not to happy about this. He is very concerned, as there has been serious talk that there will be violence. But if he wants to see the Irish side come out in my mother, he should try to stop her. I could sell tickets to that event.

At any rate, here's a quick and painful summary of how I screwed over Toni. I have decided that the reason why thinking of her, and how I handled our breakup, still hurts so much is because I really cared for her, and still do.

So, after my hook up with Nan I called Toni and set up a study date for that night. We didn't do any studying I can tell ya... but Toni studied the shit out of me. She knew right away something was up. And since I could tell that she knew, I just dove right into it.

She didn't cry. She didn't get mad. She didn't take a swing at me. But the hurt in her eyes along with her determination not to take any shit from me kinda felt like what I think hell must be like. She just reached out and touched my cheek lightly, shook her head with a painful smile, turned around and left me standing in her dorm lobby.

I can tell you the pain of that night almost made me forget Nan. But I didn't. Of course, there is a lot more to all of this including a passel of questions from LT. Guess what? I've shared all I intend to share. Good night journal!

AUGUST 29, 1963

I just heard from Liz. There was a short time when I thought my sister was never going to speak to me. She was really pissed about my breakup with Toni. For a while it looked like friendship was thicker than blood for Liz. But she reluctantly met Nan and to her credit she got it immediately. She conceded that there was room for two special girls in the life of a creep like me.

Liz was overly excited about the trip to DC. She went on and on about the size of the crowd, seeing Mahalia Jackson, Peter Paul and Mary, a dozen civil rights leaders who I had never heard of and Martin Luther King, who I had.

They had taken an overnight chartered B&O train from Cincinnati Union Terminal and arrived early the next morning into Union Station near the Capitol building. Then they walked to the Washington Monument, eventually claiming a spot on the Reflecting Pool very near the Lincoln Memorial where all of the action took place. Liz described how mom lead the way, seeming to know just where to go and what to do.

LT and I caught a little of the event yesterday on TV at the Rez. Of course, we had no idea where to look for Mom, Liz, Mir and Toni. But knowing they were somewhere in that crowd was pretty damn exciting.

Liz says that there is a movement afoot that is going to change things in America for the better. We shall see.

AUGUST 31, 1963

S o, if the trip that my mother, my sisters and my former girlfriend took to Washington DC this past week was heroic and maybe historic, the shorter trip I took yesterday can be described as pathetic and cowardly, and yet a blast.

It would not have even taken place had Coach Bo not uncharacteristically rewarded us with a short morning workout rather than the typical *knock somebody on their ass* all day torture. Nobody can figure that guy out. But by 10 AM we were finished for the Labor Day weekend and Squeaky Timmons had a plan.

We call our starting center Squeaky because when he speaks, he sounds like a combination of Mickey Mouse and Andy Devine. He kind of squeaks when he speaks.

At any rate while LT and I were dressing after our showers at Withrow Court, Squeaky threw down the gauntlet.

"How would you like to wrestle an ape and win a hundred bucks?"

he said addressing LT.

LT and I were thinking the same thing, but LT said it, "Squeaky, what the hell are you talking about?"

"Shit fire, you guys, it was in the *Oxford Press* this morning," he said, waving a copy of our local news rag in our faces.

I grabbed the paper from Squeaky and read an advertisement he had circled. Sure enough, it was there in black and white. The Dearborn County Fair in Lawrenceburg Indiana was offering the chance to wrestle an ape with a C-Note going to anyone who could pin the creature.

Well, with the afternoon off, this quickly spiraled into a Redskins outing. Before you could say "hike" we had two carsful of Miami footballers heading 35 miles south in search of a wrestling ape.

When we got to the Fair Grounds it was quickly obvious that we were in a foreign country. The uniform of the day for the army of famers on hand was oversized bib overalls and a variety of plaid shirts... mostly flannel and way too heavy for the late August heat.

Then there were ten jocks (us) trotting around like show horses in our kakis or white duck pants, crocodile infested shirts and penny loafers, while Ivy Leaguing our Joe College asses through the sawdust and mud looking for the wrestling tent and doing our best to not step in something.

Since Squeaky was the biggest and goofiest of our bunch, he stopped two *Old McDonalds* with about five teeth between them and asked if they knew where we could find the wrestling monkey. They both looked us over, spitting tobacco juice in unison, pausing so the bigger one could fart and finally pointed the way.

We weaved through the fairgrounds past a Ferris wheel, a small merry-go-round, a small trailer offering up cotton candy, two beer wagons and more hogs and goats than I had ever seen. But sure enough, we found a large tent with a huge man with tattooed arms shouting into a megaphone. His message... there was, in fact, an ape available to wrestle.

After reluctantly plopping down a buck each, we entered the tent to find a semicircle of wooden folding chairs facing a big red curtain. Most of the other patrons seemed happy, loud and drunk. Many were puffing hard on Lucky Strikes, Old Golds, Pall Malls or the farmer-preferred roll-your-own, creating a significant haze.

In the last row, far to the right side, sat four middle-aged Negroes. They were drawing a great deal of attention from most of the inebriated farm boys. The slurs were abundant and loud enough for everyone to hear. I was more concerned with LT than the mellow Negro group in the back who did not seem to be paying attention. LT has a very low tolerance for what he calls "racist bullshit."

Fortunately, before LT could get his engine revved up, the curtain opened to expose the big tattoo character from out front, holding tightly onto to a chain that was attached to a metal collar around the neck of the now famous ape.

Then something else happened. One of the less drunk farmers rose and raised his hand and said to his race-baiting compatriots, "Now, now... pipe down."

Then pointing at the four Negroes in the back of the tent, he continued, "Everybody is welcome here. Even them nigger boys back there. I bet one of them-there boys would just love to ressel their cousin, that-there ape. Which one of you boys think you can pin that monkey, and win ya a C-note?"

It was clear in the way he said "boys" and "monkey" and "ape" that he had a less than subtle agenda, while trying to create a more peaceful atmosphere where he and his drunken buddies were less likely to get arrested.

Then he turned his attention to our little posse and said, "And after one a dem boys back der get their black ass whipped, I'd sure like to see one of dem pussy-ass college boys over there give her a try."

That was enough for LT. He jumped up and shouted, "All right, you farm boys. I'll kick the ass of that gorilla and then you can all go have some shit-ass Indiana corn and go burn another cross while my friends here join me for a hundred bucks worth of steak. I'll lend you a match."

The main farmer remained calm., just smiling back at LT. But the ape was getting a little agitated tugging at the leash. I looked back over at the four negroes only to see two Indiana State Police enter the tent and sit in the back row. That sobered things up a bit. It seemed like everyone took a deep breath, as LT walked over to where the negroes were seated and said quietly to the largest of them, "Comon' friend, let's show these idiots what we're made of."

From there the ape trainer took over.

"Well folks, it looks like we have ourselves a couple of challengers for Cheeta here."

Cheeta? *What the hell*, I thought after hearing the gorilla's name for the first time. Cheeta was Tarzan's pet monkey. The creature at the front of the tent was no monkey.

As LT walked past me, he whispered in my ear, "Listen, Gunner, after I turn old Cheeta up there into hamburger, be ready to skedaddle out of here. This isn't exactly a home game."

I processed that quickly while LT and his new buddy disappeared behind a curtain.

What took place over the next ten minutes was just outta sight.

When the curtain opened it revealed an actual boxing ring with Cheeta and his master in one corner, the negro, who was a tall drink of water, in the opposite corner and a little piss-ant of a guy in the center, dressed in a referee striped shirt.

Just as if it were a match for the heavyweight title of the world, the striped runt called the opponents to the center of the ring. Cheeta, was now dressed in trunks and sported a substantial muzzle over his nose and mouth as well as pillow-size boxing mitts strapped over his hands. He did not seem pleased.

The ref actually went over a short list of rules, which clearly favored Cheeta. We also learned for the first time that the tall negro was named Rufus Burlew. In the crowd there was an abundance of race-bating chatter in spite of the presence of the Indian State cops.

The ape and his handler went back to his corner as did Rufus Burlew.

The bell clanged and the handler urged Cheeta to the middle of the ring in a not-so-gentle manner. Cheeta was making some pretty grody sounds through his muzzle.

It became quickly apparent that Cheeta only had one move and it was all he needed. The minute Rufus got near enough, Cheeta would execute a quick and powerful pendulous swing well aimed at the side of Rufus' head. It was sufficient to knock the poor guy on his ass.

I will hand it to old Rufus... he was one game negro. But no match for Cheeta and no match for the hillbilly crowd that was rooting for Cheeta. After being knocked halfway back to his birth, the ref rushed in, the trainer jerked hard on Cheeta's chain and the ape was proclaimed the winner by technical knockout. This brought every farmer in the place along with both of the cops to their feet. Rufus needed help getting to his feet as he stumbled out of the ring.

I just sat there thinking about where we would be burying LT after Cheeta finished with him. And worse yet, explaining to Schembechler how he had lost his star fullback for the season.

After about a two minute pause the curtain reopened to reveal a shirtless LT now seated in Rufus' corner, sporting a shit-eating grin like only LT could provide. The preliminaries were repeated, the smile never leaving LT's face.

Back to their respective corners they went and we awaited the bell and LT's pending death.

What happened next, I have no doubt will live on in the history of the Dearborn County Fair as well as the annals of Miami football.

The bell clanged and LT burst from his corner like a sprinter out of the starting blocks, taking Cheeta, his trainer and the ref all by surprise. LT, in a flash, was delivering punishing blows to the meaty solar plexus of the poor defenseless gorilla. LT was in so tight the poor beast couldn't throw a punch. The frustrated trainer kept jerking hard on the leash trying to create space so Cheeta could take a swing. This just spurred LT on while Cheeta began to make some very disturbing sounds.

With each tug by the ape-handler LT's punches became more persistent and Cheeta's roars more frightening.

Then I noticed that for the first time the small group of negroes and the mass of drunken farmers had bonded in their support of LT as he relentlessly ravaged King Kong. They were all on their feet cheering LT on with every new blow he threw.

Cheeta was now so agitated, that had he broken loose from his handler, he would have killed everyone in that tent. Fortunately, the little mut of a ref rushed in, raised LT's arm in the air indicating we would be needing dinner reservations to help LT spend his new small fortune.

It took the help of the two troopers to get Cheeta back to his cage. LT was given a brand new hundred-dollar bill and advised to never return to the Fair. Fair enough we all agreed.

The mighty Miami ten put our penny-loafers to work, sprinting to the parking lot. We climbed into Squeaky's beat up Chevy and LT's 1956 Ford, agreeing to reassemble at Cincinnati's Fountain Square.

By the time we reconnected by the Tyler Davidson Fountain in the middle of 5th Street, LT had done the math. One hundred dollars divided by ten hungry footballers meant ten bucks each. So, he would treat us all to a movie and popcorn at the Albee Theater, followed by dinner next door at Wiggins Restaurant.

With the new Steve McQueen film, *The Great Escape*, playing at the Albee, everyone was in. And, it was a great movie. Dinner at Wiggins' basement dive, called the Ratskeller, was even better. Most of the linemen had Wiggins' famous fried minute steak, while LT and I, being the sophisticates in the bunch, had the fried shrimp and oyster combo. When the day was through, LT had $26 left from his original $100 prize money. Quite a day it was.

september 2, 1963

Yesterday we all enjoyed our day off from Miami football by building the legend of LT the Gorilla Conqueror. By the end of the day, in some parts of the dorm, word was being spread that LT had not only pinned an ape, but had also slayed two lions, one tiger and had collected over two dozen teeth from an army of Indiana tobacco spitting hillbillies.

Today's practice was routine. But there was a lot of good energy as a result of a little rest and being in the presence of LT the giant killer.

I would like to note that I have inherited a love for the news from both of my parents. Throughout my high school years, Mom had us read the *Cincinnati Enquirer* each morning at breakfast and *The Post* when we arrived home from school. Then she had all of us gather around the TV to watch John Cameron Swasey or Chet Huntly and David Brinkley. No dinner until we had digested the news. That was the rule.

I bring this up, because tonight at 6:30, Walter Cronkite of "You Are There" fame introduced television's first half hour news program which he proudly referred to as the *CBS Evening News*. Now this doubled the time of any news show up until today. I'm not sure how they plan to fill that extra 15 minutes. But tonight, they did so by running an interview with President Kennedy, the one man on earth that my mother might leave my father for. But then she wouldn't do that to Jackie. Mom loves her too.

And it was thanks to Mom that I was aware of this news expansion, as she had read all about it in the *TV Guide*. That little baby has been showing up every Tuesday at our Roselawn front door since 1955, roughly speaking.

Now this is all a mix of fancy facts that didn't need to be recorded here in my journal. But I'm using a ballpoint pen. And that is fairly indelible. So, this entry is here to stay as an indication that I had a pretty boring day. Good night!

september 7, 1963

I'm a little ashamed to admit that I have avoided any attempt to record the goings on in my awarding winning life since Monday. And other than football and our usual juvenile behavior, this has been a rather uneventful week. The truth is, I can get a little lazy at times.

Today is Saturday and we had another full pad scrimmage this morning while listening to Bo rant about how shitty we are when it comes to the game of football. But as LT said to me on our walk back to the dorm, "Fuck him. He's the coach and its his job to make us something better than shitty. We were 8-2-1 and went to the Tangerine Bowl last year under Johnny Pont. Nothing shitty about that."

Bo's been riding LT's ass pretty hard because the big guy is the team offensive Captain and a stud All-Conference fullback. And I can tell you, nobody works harder than LT. I dare anyone in the Mid-America Conference to find a better team leader. So, I'm with LT... fuck Schembechler!

On a more positive note, after the scrimmage, LT and I came back to our room and listened to the Cincinnati Reds, as described by the great Waite Hoyt, beat the New York Mets, a group of clowns masquerading as a major league baseball team, by a modest 4-2 margin. Hoyt also informed LT, me and the 50 or so other people probably listening, that today's game between the Washington Senators and the Cleveland Indians was considered to be the 100,000th game played in Major League Baseball. In true Hoyt fashion he also shared that the very first game was played on May 4, 1871 between the Fort Wayne Kekiongas and Cleveland Forest City.

LT suggested that my fastball would have scared the holy shit out of those 1871 bearded ballplayers. Then he asked what the hell was a Kekiongas? I had no answer to that one.

After the game we tuned into WSAI to listen to some rock and roll, which included The Angels new hit, "My Boyfriend's Back." Now that struck a real chord, because on Monday my girlfriend will be back. Brooksie is scheduled to show up on campus sometime midday in the family limo. I don't want to get into the limo nonsense except to admit that to have a gorgeous girlfriend whose father breeds race horses and gets squired around in a big ass black Lincoln with a driver in a monkey suit and a funny hat, is a little intimidating.

The big topic of conversation at dinner tonight, other than what a prick our new coach is, centered on the official opening of the Professional Football Hall of Fame in Canton Ohio. Nobody can figure out why it has been built in Canton. But then, the baseball Hall of Fame is in some upstate New York burg called Cooperstown. New York and Chicago weren't available? But what the hell do I know?

september 9, 1963

Two things of note happened today. The first kinda finished setting the table for my senior year, and is a big goddamn deal, while the second is a football piece of news that won't get any real coverage, but should. First and foremost, Brooksie is back on campus. She rolled up to Wells Hall on Spring Street in one of her Daddy's two limousines around 4 o'clock. Wells is a three-story Ladies Dorm smack in the middle of campus, where Nan will be bunking with her best girl pal, Jan Marney, for the next nine months. Now, *Jan-Mar*, as LT has dubbed her, is one interesting cookie. While Brooksie is more of a southern belle, Jan is one hot heart stopper from Atlanta, and about as subtle as a freight train. That makes her LT's type. After practice today I hustled my Irish butt over to Wells because I'm in love. LT led the way because he's in lust. Its fair to say, indelicately, that LT and I will both be scoring off of the football field before the week is out. My scoring with Nan is a relatively new thing, while scoring with Jan-Mar for LT is just another Monday. Ya see, LT has himself a small harem on campus. The only reason he was in a rush today to reconnect with Jan-Mar is that the rest of his entourage hasn't arrived back in Oxford yet.LT doesn't particularly like the word harem. He prefers to say that he has a dozen or so of Miami's most attractive coeds on retainer. He's a funny guy, my roommate.

At any rate LT and I rewarded the return of Nan and Jan-Mar by taking them to the Rez for a toasted roll and a coke. There are just certain campus traditions that must not be ignored. And it was there that I learned of the second piece of football news. LT had heard from our teammate, Cecil Thomson, that a former Grambling kick-off returner and halfback named Stone Johnson had died yesterday after fracturing his vertebra two weeks ago in a preseason game playing for the Kansas City Chiefs. Cecil's older brother, Marcus had played with Johnson at Grambling the all-Negro college down south somewhere. More importantly Johnson had run the 200 meter in the Rome Olympics three years ago. At one time he had held the world record. And now he is gone.

This was generally an unspoken subject in college football. Guys weren't supposed to die playing the game. But LT and I knew Johnson wasn't the first and clearly wouldn't be the last. Yet none of us fretted about it. Like so many other tragic things in life, most football players just assumed that this was something that only happened to someone else. But LT told me that he felt badly for Cecil and that he could see both the grief and the fear in Cecil's eyes when he told LT about his brother's ex-teammate. Cecil is a tight end and one of four negroes on our team this year.

LT said to me as we wolfed down our toasted rolls, "B-3, we need to keep an eye on Cecil to see how this will affect him long term. He is a great player and we need him to keep his head on straight."

I agreed and we returned our attention to the two finest looking women in the building, doing so with equal doses of affection and desire. "My girlfriend's back," I hummed to myself as Brooksie squeezed my arm tightly. I had been singing that damned song since I heard it on WSAI Saturday night. Is there going to be trouble? I wondered. Nah... not with this sweet chick.

Rest in peace, Stone Johnson.

September 13, 1963

I t is Friday the 13ᵗʰ. Watch out for black cats and stay away from ladders, less you walk under one. What a crock. I don't buy any of that superstitious shit. But on the other hand, I do always double-tie my cleats (football or baseball) and I never step on the sideline chalk (football) or the baseline chalk (baseball)... EVER!! That would just be asking for trouble.

Let me say that I have always loved football. But I've been in a serious football funk so far this year. I have tried to analyze it as best I can. I'm just not enjoying it.

It could be Schembechler. He's a pain in the ass. And, I loved Johnny Pont. But LT thinks Bo is the answer to our prayers. And truthfully, I think I'm the problem, not Coach.

Then it could be related, in large part, to Brooksie. Well, not so much Nan herself, but rather the fact that her family is loaded. And, I sense her parents don't exactly see me as the son-in-law of their dreams.

As it turns out, Lawrence Brooks, Nan's father, started making some little gadgets for the auto industry in the late-thirties. He then parlayed that modest little factory in Lexington into something huge, by converting to airplane parts for the war effort. Next thing you know, old Larry was one rich sumbitch much to the delight of his wife, the former Miss Kentucky, Francis Middleton Brooks... or as I like to call her behind her back "Our Miss Brooks." But believe me, it's "Mrs. Brooks" to her face.

I have a name for old Larry too... and its not Larry. I call him "Bags", as in money *bags*. Brooksie has come to embrace the new moniker for her old man. At first, she would just roll her eyes and give off with a rye grin. But now, if *Bags* isn't in the room, it's *Bags* all around.

There's no question about where Nan gets her looks. Our Miss Brooks (Francis) is one hot 45-year-old. She's a whole bunch better looking than Eve Arden I can tell ya. A bit more like one of those Gabor sisters. I half expect her to greet me with that thick Zsa Zsa Hungarian accent, "Hellooo Daaahling."

But instead, what comes out is more like Minnie Pearl, "Well howdy their Sugar. Ain't you just da swaatest thang?"

While her twang might enlist the term "Red Neck," her persona screams sophistication and elegance

At any rate, the Brookses now own a sprawling horse farm not far from Keenland Race Track. It runs along Route 60 west of downtown Lexington. And, they are deeply emersed in Lexington society not to mention the Republican Party. I haven't shared that last part with Mom yet. John Kennedy is Mom's man (in case you haven't heard, he's Irish).

As comfortable as I am with Brooksie, l was like a fish flopping around on the floor of a bass boat gasping for my last breath, the two times I have visited "Brooks Ridge Farm" this summer. Yes, you read that right. My girlfriend lives at some fancy pants horse farm with slave walls and a big-ass sign over the gate that guards against riff raff like me from entering uninvited. And her father's new ambition is to breed a Kentucky Derby winner. He probably expects to be Governor of Kentucky some day also, if they ever get around to electing Republicans in the Bluegrass State.

Which leads to another reason I may be in this funk. My parents seem to love Nan. Even my two sisters are coming around despite what I did to Toni. And, yes, I still can't shake the guilt of that little episode.

To continue this self-therapy, I have to admit football this season has become merely a diversion to the long wait ahead before I can take to the mound again next spring and get to what I hope will be the big payday next June.

To tell the truth, all of this has me more nervous than a whore in church and feeling like a lost ball in tall weeds.

And speaking of Toni, she has moved on. Everywhere I turn, someone is reminding me that she has hooked up with basketball star, Skip Bolden. Skip is an All-Conference guard, President of Beta Theta Pi, and all-round good guy.

I know, this shit isn't supposed to trouble me. I traded Toni in for a new model. So, what the hell is bothering me? Classes start next week. Maybe that will help.

As I said, it's Friday the 13th.

September 17, 1963

W ell, the first day of classes for my senior year has arrived.
I start this morning at nine with *Macro Economic*s in Upham Hall. Then at ten, I have to skedaddle over to Hughes Hall for *American Lit, 1900-Present*. At one o'clock it is *U.S. Diplomatic History* as presented by the renowned Professor Richard Jellison, also at Hughes Hall. Then repeat that schedule every Wednesday and Friday.

On Tuesdays and Thursdays, it's morning only. Starting at 8:30 with *Statistics* to fulfill a requirement... not too excited about this one, but ya gotta do what you gotta do. Right? Then from 10-11:30, it will be *Modern German History* (oh boy... featuring big names like Bismarck, Wilhelm, Hitler and Adenauer). That thriller will be in Irvin Hall.

All together that adds up to 15 credit hours for this Fall Semester.

Five spiral ring notebooks stand ready. Let's hope I am.

And to solidify our growing love, Brooksie has enrolled in both my *American Lit* and my *Modern German History* classes. That will make studying together more fun. Yet it might add some additional pressure. I have done very well in the classroom my first three years here at Miami. But if I allow those two classes to evolve into a competition, I'll go 0 for 2. Brooksie might be the brightest person I've ever been around. About the only thing she will choose over me is studying. For her, a "B" just isn't an option. Oh well, it wasn't just her blue eyes and perfect tits that I fell for.

As they say down on Brooks Ridge Farm… "We're off to the races."

Macro Economics, here I come!

September 20, 1963

W ell, it's been a good first week of classes. What I can say without reservation, is that there will be a lot of reading this semester. But I can read. So be it.

Tomorrow we finally kickoff (pun intended) the football season against Xavier University with a home game here in Oxford. The most interesting thing for LT and me about Xavier is that they are coached by Eddie Biles. Biles was the first head coach at our alma mater, Woodward High School when they moved from downtown Cincinnati to the new yellow brick building on Reading Road in the suburb of Bond Hill in 1953. Thus, it is now known as *New Woodward* (Go Bulldogs).

Biles won the first game New Woodward ever played in the fall of 1954, upsetting Xavier (High School, not University). And he did it without any seniors, because there were none that first year. Then he lost nine straight.

By the time LT and I made it to the varsity, Biles was long gone, coaching the XU Freshman team. Now LT is Miami's Star Fullback and Co-Captain, I'm the place kicker and here comes Eddie Biles and Xavier. We should kick their collective asses, if Schembechler doesn't screw it up.

Tonight, it's an early movie with Brooksie, and tomorrow when my right toes lift the ball off of the tee, the football season is on.

September 21, 1963

{{{

W ell, Schembechler screwed the pooch, along with our center, Squeaky Timmons.

Let's start with Bo. He obviously read this morning's *Cincinnati Enquirer* piece that said, "Miami has a strong experienced offensive line, the kind that Schembechler likes for his style of power football."

I say that because all we did all day was run the football alla Woody Hayes.

Now, in Tommy Campbell, we have a guy who can literally throw a football 70 yards with ease. And he throws short bullet passes with the accuracy of an Annie Oakley six shooter. So, of course, Bo decides to run the ball straight ahead. Only because LT specializes in knocking big people on their asses, and our right halfback, Scotty Fowler is more slippery than a greased pig, were we able to go up early, 12 – 0, with LT and Scotty each scoring a touchdown.

Now, it should have been 14 – 0. Except that I failed to make both extra points. This is where Squeaky comes in. On my first attempt, like always, I am focused on the kicking tee, waiting for Tommy Campbell to spot the ball down for me. That didn't happen. Instead, the ball came high and hard and hit me squarely in the chops. First of all, that shit hurts. Second, that shit draws blood. And third, I can't kick an extra point for shit without a football to kick.

I was almost as pissed off as Bo.

Then after Scotty Fowler's crowd thrilling 52-yard touchdown run around end, we huddled again. Tommy looked at Squeaky in the huddle and said, "hey Squeak-Man, ya think you can keep this snap somewhere in the stadium?"

Squeaky confidently promised to hit Tommy smack in the hands, then proceeded to snap the ball five feet over Tommy's head. Without a ladder, Campbell didn't have a prayer.

I sprinted back about 15 yards and was able to cover the ball. Then I was covered by half of the Xavier team, leaving me feeling that I should be searching the turf for half of my teeth.

After scraping myself up from that beautiful Miami Field lawn, I decided it would be wise to locate Bo and to head for the opposite side of the bench. That was easy enough as Schembechler had Squeaky by the face guard leaving our poor center scanning the stadium looking for an insurance agent.

Scotty's exciting TD provided the last points to be scored by the Redskins this afternoon. Xavier scored three easy touchdowns in the second half. As they had a normal center, they also scored all of the points-after, and we had lost our opener to an inferior Xavier Musketeer football team.

Since all Bo decided to do in the second half was have Tommy hand the ball off to LT, my roomie took a beating and our receivers got the day off. After Bo rearranged the furniture in our post-game locker room and sent Squeaky back out to practice snaps, LT limped his beat-up ass to the whirlpool for a major soak.

I was left with a fat lip. No whirlpool therapy for me. And no mouth-to-mouth therapy with Nan either. Fuck football!

september 22, 1963

S o, yesterday's game result provides a couple of illustrations about two of my closest relationships... those with LT and Brooksie.

Nobody in our locker room (including Bo) was more pissed off about losing to Xavier than LT and me. But the more important thing is that by the time we each took a half a dozen steps out of Withrow Court, we were both over it. After all, it was only a game of football, not the game of life. That approach has been basic in both LT and me for a long time.

It has always been this way. When it's over, it's over. Win or lose, we chalk it up to experience and move on. The game is over, let the fun begin. Be happy. We will be ready for the next one. This is a big part of why our friendship is so strong. We have perspective.

Then there's Brooksie. She understands and appreciates my ability to move on from success or failure with equal enthusiasm. And I know why she loves this. Her father, the Big Money Bags of Lexington, is not like that at all. He refuses to lose. Just won't stand for it and cannot get over it. This has bruised Nan over the entirety of her 20 years on planet Earth.

So, last night, when I picked her up in her dorm lobby, she stood there with a welcoming smile that kind of said, *fuck Xavier, let's go have some fun.*

And that's what we did. Off we went in LT's hidden Ford, bound for the Dixie Inn in Hamilton, LT at the wheel and Jan-Mar riding shotgun. When we arrived, we had a modest dinner and then Brooksie and I feasted on each other for the next eight hours or so. And some fine feast is my Brooksie girl.

Nan and I had been very slow with the physical side of our relationship. But it has evolved and is now hotter than a stolen tamale... emphasis on the spice.

Nan had signed out for the night, claiming to be going to Dayton with her roommate, Jan-Mar, who is actually from Atlanta, and was secretly down the hall with LT in room 116 of the Dixie Inn. I had plopped down six bucks for room 110.

After a quick breakfast this morning at Perkins Pancake House we all took the half hour drive back to Oxford.

Now, I was going to leave this part out, but here goes. After our second round of sexual gymnastics last night, Nan said those three little words that can give you goose bumps, or, on the other hand, cause you to shit a brick. For me it was bumps over bricks. And, out loud, without hesitation, "I love you too," popped right out of my wounded mouth. I suppose part of me had been wandering what had taken so long. And that same part of me is glad that she said it first. At any rate, we're not shopping for fine China and linens yet.

LT and I are both well aware that Schembechler will put us through hell this week as we prepare for Marshall. Friday, the Thundering

Herd come to town and on Saturday we plan to kick their hick asses. Yee Haw!!

september 25, 1963

Way back in the 7th grade LT and I made a pack… we were going to make something of ourselves, we weren't going to take any shit from anyone and, most importantly, we would have no secrets and always look out for each other. As LT stated, "Billy Boy, that's what real friendship looks like."

And, we haven't wavered once on that pact.

The reason I bring this up is that LT and I have been talking a lot lately about girls. I had told him about the "I love you" sideshow that Brooksie and I had over the weekend. And, to my surprise, he told me he was starting to have serious feelings for Jan-Mar.

Now that is big news. LT probably has had more girlfriends in three years at Miami than our whole defense has fingers, toes, ears and noses. As I like to say, LT has more notches on his pecker than Hop-a-Long Cassidy has on his six-shooter. That's just how LT has always looked at women… objects to be conquered, then discarded

He even has classifications for women based solely on their appearance. Ninety percent of the ladies we bump into are not even worthy of a rating. But those who are, have obtained one of the following:

- *Quickie*

- *All-nighter*

- *Weekender*

- *Seven days somewhere warm*

- *One month on a remote island*

- ...and the unattainable... *Will you marry me?*

From the get-go Jan-Mar was a good for a week in a warm climate. Yeah buddy, she's a real looker. But last night he admitted if it wasn't for football and classes, he could disappear for a month... Jan-Mar in tow.

And, clearly, I'm having those same kind of feelings for Nan. Though sometimes I think she would run off to Reno with me just to spite her mother. Her mom is kind of what you might expect a beauty queen to be... full of herself. And I just found out on my last trip to the family horse farm, that not only was she Miss Kentucky 1940, but she was third runner-up in the Miss America contest that year. Now, one thing I am sure of, is that you are more likely to find Brooksie trying to milk a pig, than to see her entering a beauty contest.

But I'm way off the track. The main point is, thanks to our 7th grade pack, LT and I are talking about going beyond the "shack-up" stage. It is starting to feel like we are starring in "Gentlemen Prefer Blondes."

We better get our heads back to football. And for me, baseball, too.

september 27, 1963

I t's actually been a good week of practice. Bo has spent a lot of time on our passing game. Anyone with a brain knows that throwing a few passes will open up our running game, meaning that Scotty and LT should be more productive. We shall see.

Quizzes and tests have started in the classroom, to assure we are not just listening but also learning. I can proudly report that I have provided strong evidence that the knowledge is sticking to my brain. So far, it's all A's for B-3. Or as they say in the Space Program... All is *A-OK*!

Tomorrow, I have more than Marshall to worry about. Bags and Miss Kentucky will be in attendance, probably in the hope that that their daughter's new plaything (me) will screw up. Tonight, they are staying at the Terrace Plaza Hotel in Cincinnati and dining at the four-star Pigalle's while sucking back extra dry martinis and dining on duck l'orange and beef Wellington... La de fucking da!

As to tomorrow, Squeaky better have his shit together on those PATs. LT is confident in both Squeaky and the Redskins. He says the Marshall boys are better at fucking their cousins than football. Bring 'em on.

september 28, 1963

There's something about when the Redskins run onto the field before a home game that is euphoric. I know it's corny, but it's true. At Miami we are led from the northern endzone by Jim Cooley, or Hiawopbop as he is known, fully regaled in Miami Indian garb aboard a beautiful Palomino pony, riding bareback and waving a tommyhawk. To be in the middle of that pack of footballers as the crowd screams and the band loudly blast the Miami fight song for the ten people who know the words:

Love and honor to Miami
Our college old and grand
Proudly we shall ever hail thee
Over all the land. □

Alma Mater now we praise thee
Sing joyful we lay
Love and honor to Miami
Forever and a day!

Now in my book that's goosebump stuff. Sure, anything that has *thee* in it twice is a bit too much. And I have no idea what *Sing joyful we lay* means. But I can tell you my pulse rate goes way up between the endzone and the bench. It's a magical 50 yards.

Out front, as always were co-captains LT (AKA Chief) and Red Smith, our All-Conference linebacker. I could tell you what color Red's hair is, but if you needed help with that, you should probably burn this missive and go back to the funny pages.

On our runout today, I was nervously aware of the presence of Bags and Miss Kentucky in the stands. I knew exactly where they were sitting because I got them the tickets. We can't have them depleting their vast fortune on $15 box seats to a Miami football game.

Miami Information Director, Bob Kurz, got me the best tickets he could lay his hands on. Bob's a cool guy. A 1958 graduate of Miami, Bob is pure Redskin. It was Kurz who first dubbed Miami as "The Cradle of Coaches."

And its true. The coaching lineage at MU is extraordinary, including Red Blake (Army), Woody Hayes (Ohio State), Paul Brown (Cleveland Browns), Sid Gillman (Cincinnati and Los Angeles Rams), Paul Dietzel (LSU), Ara Parseghian (Northwestern), Web Eubank, (Baltimore Colts), my old coach Johnny Pont (now at Yale), not to mention Smokey Alston (Brooklyn and LA Dodgers).

That little list has produced several National Championships and a couple of World Series wins. Just another reason to love good old MU and my favorite ticket agent, Bob Kurz.

The game started well with the Skins marching right down the field on six completed passes from Tommy Campbell, two first down scampers by Scotty Fowler, capped off by a two-yard plunge by LT for the score.

Better news yet... Squeaky hit Tommy right in the hands and my PAT kick was dead center perfect... See that Money Bags?

Unfortunately, after that opening drive, the game turned boring with a capital BORE. There were more punts than pass completions on both sides of the ball. After Tommy threw an interception for a Marshall score, Bo went back to the running game. I love LT. But running him three times off guard followed by a punt isn't the way to score in the Mid-America Conference.

In the second half we recovered a fumble that led to a Scotty Fowler TD on an option around end. Again, Squeaky, Tommy and I were in perfect concert and my kick made it Skins 14 - Hillbillies 7.

With the clock ticking down to our first win of the season, when Bo should have been giving the ball to LT on every play, he decides Scotty should have a turn. Bo is an equal opportunity coach.

Bad call. Scotty got popped hard, up in the air goes the pigskin falling into the arms of the Marshall safety who took it to paydirt. PAT was good and we sulked back to our locker room with a tie.

Another blown chance by Bo. There's already talk of hanging him in effigy. I can't think of a defense.

I polished off the day by meeting Nan, Bags and Our Miss Brooks for a quick Lincoln limo drive back to Cincinnati and dinner at our town's other renowned eatery, The Maisonette. Bags loves his French food, so I've been told. Now, I have lived in Cincinnati my whole life without ever setting foot in either the Maisonette or Pigalle's. It's not in our price range and dad still hasn't forgiven the French for caving so fast in WWII.

But Brooksie is my girl and the baggage that comes with that is da Bags and da beauty queen. Pass the caviar.

In spite of the fact that I couldn't read half of the menu, dinner was actually really good. Who knew I would like snails... sorry, *escargot*. I ordered the Sole Meuniere, mostly because I recognized Sole as fish. I still don't know what Meuniere is or how to pronounce it, but our waiter understood when I said, "I'll have the sole."

Bags and Miss K ordered something that they set on fire tableside. While I was looking for a phone to call the fire department, the blaze went out and the Brookes ate what was left. The Caesar salad that Bags ordered for the table was a big production and I took a ration of shit from Our Miss Brooks for setting the little fishes to the side. Dessert was also set on fire but the ashes were quite tasty.

Around 10:30 the Brookes, with Nan in tow, walked the two blocks back to their hotel after tucking me into their limo driven by a hansom well-uniformed chap named Jerome, for the ride back to my home in Roselawn. I normally don't use the word "chap", but after dinner at the Maisonette, "chap" seems appropriate.

I can only wonder how much more Bags might have spent tonight had we beat Marshall. The one thing I'm pretty sure of is that I don't want to be rich. While I'm hoping to get a big bonus next spring, whatever I get will be pocket change for Bags. Really big money is not for me.

When I walked in on my mother, who was busy reading the latest "Readers Digest," she asked if I had a good day. Tying an inferior Marshall football team, watching the Brookses try to burn down the Maisonette and being served a salad with tiny fish on top, was not what I would call a good day. But I lied and told her it was just peachy keen. What the hell... somehow, I'm still crazy about Brooksie. It's hard to believe she was raised by Scrooge McPrick and Miss Kentucky 1940.

Like me, Nan seems to prefer Tuffy's over the Maisonette and toasted rolls over crepes suzette. Fingers crossed. I hope I'm not missing something.

september 29, 1963

One thing I am certain of is that my mother and father truly love each other. Dad often calls mom, "mo mhuirnín dílis," which is Celtic for "my own true love." And he pronounces it with that perfect Irish brough that he can conjure up, that makes it come out, "mu voor-neen deelish."

I heard him say that to her in the kitchen this morning. And though mom is half Irish, she always comes back with the Jewish half of her, "You're such a Meshuggeneh, but I love you too, Bubbelah."

Frankly, there is such an ease in their relationship that Mir, Liz and I all agree we have been truly blessed when it comes to parents. We hit the jackpot.

So, this morning I am mentally contrasting that with the Duke and Duchess of Brooksdom. Mom and Dad are devoted to each other, while Bags and Miss 1940 seem to be devoted to what they see in the mirror. And, therein lies the riddle of Nan. Her sweetness defies her parentage.

But back to Mom and Dad, I must say, there is one way Dad can immediately piss off Mom. All it takes is one of his now famous limericks. He has two types... clean and dirty.

An example of Dad going clean might be:

> *There once was a man from Nantucket,*
> *Who kept all his cash in a bucket.*☐
> *His daughter, named Nan*
> *Ran away with a man,*
> *And, as for the bucket, Nan took it!*

With that one, Mom will just roll her eyes and say, "enough already." And I should point out we are hearing a lot of that one since I started dating Nan.

But when Dad goes long with what Mom calls his "toilet limericks." it's a different story. And sure enough, this morning over pancakes he shared this:

> *There once was a young man from Kent*
> *With a dick so long, it was bent*
> *To save himself trouble*
> *He's put it in double,*
> *And then instead of coming he went*

That little beaut got him a crack to the back of the head and a stern warning that he might be fixing his own dinner. He got the message and asked Mir to bring us up to date on the first month of her Senior year at good old Woodward High School. As I already knew, the

Bulldog eleven were off to a better start than the Redskins (Sis Boom Ba!).

After breakfast I dialed up LT to secure my ride back to campus. Fortunately, he had come home last night to lick his wounds, or rather to have Sally Ransom lick them for him. Sally is part of LT's old Woodward harem and stands permanently at the ready position. Unknown by Sally, to LT, she is a perpetual *Quickie*.

On the drive back to Oxford, LT came clean. He's just not ready for any real commitment to Jan-Mar. He just likes girls way too much to devote his affection to any one of the species, including the drop-dead gorgeous Jan-Mar. She has been demoted again to a *Weekender*.

One final thing to note. This journal thing is demanding too much of my attention. Between my classes, football, Brooksie and the ever-present impatience of waiting for baseball season, I'm a bit fried. Maybe a weekly summary might make more sense for now. Up next... Western Michigan. Kalamazoo, here we come.

OCTOBEr 6, 1963

W ell, we finally got a win yesterday. Western Michigan might be the worst team we will play this year. While we didn't exactly blow them out of Waldo Stadium, LT ran for 142 yards and two touchdowns, one of his best days ever at Miami. I had a perfect day with the old right foot, converting 3 points-after and nailing two field goals... one from 45-yards out. Bo wasn't going to allow me to try that one, but assistant coach Bobby Galat, talked him into it during a well-timed timeout. I nailed that sumbitch, dead center perfect. The final score was 27-19, and the bus ride back to Oxford was raucous.

Bo gave LT the game ball and me a pat on the head. And we finally learned that he actually knew how to smile.

We arrived back on campus well after midnight. So, all of the school's female talent were securely tucked inside their dormitories, jailed by the Miami mandatory women's curfew.

Nothing pisses off my sister Liz more than female students at Miami living under a curfew system, that does not apply to male students. Like it or not, the ladies must live in dormitories, and must adhere to curfews. So, on Monday through Thursday they lock the doors at 10 PM. On Friday and Saturday, it is Cinderella midnight. And on Sunday, the jail keeper locks 'em up at 11.

Liz likes to point out that a vastly more mature twenty-one-year-old legally adult woman can be locked up at 10 PM, while an eighteen-year-old *child-boy* can wonder around Oxford at will.

Yep, that shit gets my sister riled up. As Dad says... "Life ain't fair."

At any rate, we got our win yesterday and it was a very good week in class. So far, all I have to do is read, as assigned, and the good grades seem to follow. And ignoring this journal this past week, allowed more time at the end of each day to do the reading.

If your following baseball (and you're a fool if you don't) the World Series started this week. My man Sandy Koufax struck out a record 15 Yankees in a Game 1 Dodger win at Yankee Stadium. There are some who are expecting me to become a right-handed Koufax. I sure don't want to think about that. This week, I'm just a place kicker in the Mid-America Conference and baseball is six months off.

Then there's Brooksie. Since our French dinner a week ago, she has been very attentive. It is clear that she is concerned about my reaction to Bags and da Queen. And I have to admit they do provide new meaning to the term, "Looney Tunes."

Nan actually told me on Wednesday, on our way back to her 10 o'clock lockup, that she was very jealous of Liz, Mir and me, wishing she had parents like ours. What do you say to that? Like a coward, I lied and said her mom and dad weren't that bad. Frankly, I try not to look too far ahead, or I start envisioning Thanksgivings in Lexington among horses prancing outside the dining room picture window and caviar dressing.

All I can say is Brooksie is one fine piece of womanhood. If they want to serve the cranberry sauce on fire, count me in for the cranberry soup... I think.

OCTOBER 13, 1963

\(\langle\)

W e are on a roll. It was another road win yesterday for the Redskins. This time we kicked the collective asses of the Kent State Golden Flashes by a lopsided score of 30-8. They didn't show much flash at Memorial Stadium. The only thing they won was best band playing the National Anthem. But then, they were the only band playing the National Anthem.

After Scottie scored a 65-yard TD around the right side on our first drive, LT punched in two more scores. I was delighted to provide all three points after, plus three more field goals. I sense that Bo is falling in love with me.

Speaking of love, Nan has laid that pronouncement on me out loud a few more times. And I love her too. For some reason it's just harder for me to get it out. That fact is starting to concern my perfect girl. So, I've asked LT to help me. I ask him to just blurt out "I love you" arbitrarily so that I can train to react right back with an "I love you too."

Now, LT wasn't too keen on this at first. But then he saw the humor in it. Now, he will spit it out any chance he can in order to embarrass me. Let me tell you, this doesn't play well in the locker room. But LT thinks it's a hoot.

After several days of his shenanigans, he said something that made sense. LT suggested, "B-3 my man, I think the smartest thing you can do is say it first. You know, when you get into some heavy snoofing outside her dorm each night, beat her to the love punch. Whata ya gotta loose?"

It made sense. So, I tried it on Wednesday night and she lit up like a Christmas tree. When you say it first, it's official. Let's head to the jewelry store? Maybe, not yet.

I don't know anyone funnier than my pal LT. To loosen things up in the locker room this week he organized a new little game. He calls it, "The Sammy Davis, Jr. Medley."

In case you hadn't heard Sammy Davis lost an eye a while back... a fact that is quite clear when he appears on TV. So, LT suggested that we find songs with the word "eyes" in the title and change it to "eye."

So far, the list is meager and as follows:

- *The Eye of Texas is Upon You*

- *I Only Have Eye for You*

- *Green Eye*

- *Can't Take My Eye off You*

- *Smoke Gets in Your Eye*

But it did its job. It has loosened things up, and we're headed to Northwestern and a likely ass whoopin'. Nothing funny about that.

OCTOBER 20, 1963

W ell, I guess it wasn't an ass whoopin', but we got our butts kicked 37-6. It was a perfect Midwest autumn day yesterday in Evanston. The trip was better than the game. We left Oxford Friday morning and arrived in Downtown Chicago a little after three in the afternoon.

Nobody can figure how Bo pulled it off, but we stayed at the Chicago Athletic Association Hotel on Michigan Avenue. This is an exclusive men's club in the heart of the city that looks out onto Grant Park and Lake Michigan beyond.

Normally it's gentlemen members only. Now I don't know any real gentlemen on our team (other than LT and me, of course). But Bo secured 20 rooms and a team dinner up on the second floor in a room that had three fireplaces.

There's a plaque in the lobby that says the building's facade was modeled after the Doge Palace in Venice. Most of the guys on the team assumed that was a fancy dog house for dogs owned by rich Italians. Not too many intellectuals in the game of football.

At any rate, we boarded the team bus outside the dog house Saturday morning for the drive up Lake Michigan to Evanston. I have been to Chicago a couple of times with my family. But we mostly went to the museums and to Wrigley Field and Comiskey Park. I had no idea of the wealth in Northern Chicago. First there was a long line of fancy apartment buildings along Lake Shore Drive, each with a uniformed doorman. Then we drove through a string of neighborhoods with stately mansions that might even be out of Money Bags' price-range.

Ryan Field proved that there is a serious difference between the Big Ten and the Mid-American conferences. Then Northwestern proved it again on the field. Yours truly was two for two in the field goal department (not nearly enough). The drive back to Oxford was long and quiet.

Next up is Ohio University, who will be in Oxford for Homecoming weekend. I have a date. LT, as always will be picking one out of the hat with full confidence that whomever he picks will be available.

OCTOBER 27, 1963

{{{

W ell, it was close yesterday, but we lost again to the Ohio U Bobcats, in a squeaker, by a score of 13-10.

Homecoming weekend is a big deal at Miami. We kick it off on Friday night with a big-ass bonfire at our practice site, Cook Field. The Sigma Alpha Epsilon fraternity boys really stepped up this year. They recently refurnished their frat-house at the end of Withrow Street. Thus, they brought three truckloads of old beds, desks and chairs creating a pile so tall it was really dangerous. But a couple of drunken brothers topped the stack off with a large chair. Jim Cooley aboard his handsome Palomino steed road wildly around the pile with a torch in hand, eventually bending over to ignite the twenty-foot-high Mount SAE. That sucker went up in flames like none I've seen in my four years here.

And I'll tell you this. Jim looks a lot more like Jeronimo than Chuck Connors did in that movie last year. But then Jeronimo was an Apache. The most famous Miami Indian was a cat named Little Turtle. I looked it up. They're not about to make a movie called "Little Turtle." Who would star in that? Pinky Lee? Here I go again, getting off the subject.

Before the lighting ceremony, they introduce the football team. Bo got seriously booed, while LT, speaking for the team, and predicting we would be having Bobcat burgers for lunch on Saturday afternoon, was roundly cheered. The bonfire that Hiawopbop had so proficiently lit, left a huge scorched scar on the Cook Field turf. But in a way it was a slow year, with only one couple being arrested by the Oxford Police for having sex under a couple of large blankets. Just stupid freshmen. Everybody knows the golf course is the designated area for outdoor sex.

Yesterday morning I ran over to Nan's dorm to deliver a large mum corsage, another Miami tradition. She offered to kiss my right foot for good luck, but I settled for a couple of lip smashes instead. And, oh yeah, LT was with me to deliver a mum to the lottery winner, the beautiful Jan-Mar. I think the fix was in on the drawing, as every piece of paper in the hat had Jan-Mar's name on it.

At 11:30 we were on the field for our pre-game warmup. It was a Chamber of Commerce day, as if Norman Rockwell had painted this piece of autumn perfection. With white, and especially yellow mums, adorning the left mammary of a majority of the female fans, the crowd was happy and partisan.

In his pre-game "win one for the Gipper" talk, Bo reminded us that Bobcat coach, Bill Hess had promised never to lose to Miami as long as Bo was at the helm of the Redskins. And so yesterday we saw that he was good to his word. Bo and Hess had both served as assistant coaches for Woody Hayes at Ohio State. Rather than friendship resulting from that collaboration, they absolutely detested each other. So, that kind of set the table for the afternoon battle.

As far as I'm concerned everything about yesterday was perfect with the exception of our coach's strategy. Bo was all Woody Hayes personified. While Hess had a plan that looked like he had never heard of Hayes. We ran the ball. They passed the ball. On paper, we have the better quarterback by far. But Tommy Campbell can't produce points if all he does is hand off the ball.

LT ran the ball 28 times for a total of 63 yards and an absolute beating by the OU defense. They knew he was running the ball so they just keyed on him. Most of the afternoon, LT couldn't even generate a cloud of dust. Tommy was permitted to throw the ball only nine times. One of those was a screen pass to LT that went for a 26-yard touchdown. My kick was good.

My highlight film came late in the third quarter when Bo allowed me to try a field goal from 48 yards out. I split the uprights with 10 yards to spare.

Our defense did a great job holding OU from the end zone. But they converted two short field goals, one with less than a minute to play, and we lost our chance to beat the best team in the conference. Hess had kept his word.

At the moment, most Miami fans are not Schembechler fans. But my pal LT and I continue to do our part. Oh well. At least we had a dance to attend.

The Homecoming dance, like always, was held in Withrow Court. The Event Committee had landed the Les Elkhart Orchestra. They filled the gym with good dance music that was a little long on Big Band and woefully short on Rock and Roll. As such, there was a lot of slow dances. No complaints from Brooksie on that front. LT was pretty beat up, but he put on his best duds and kept Jan-Mar on the dance floor all night.

You're suppose to win your homecoming game. I looked it up. Apparently Schembechler didn't. Only good news... LT and I are the two leading Redskin scorers, half way through the season. Is there any way we can get Johnny Pont back from Yale?

November 3, 1963

W ell, Bo finally cut Tommy Campbell loose. We threw the ball more than twenty times yesterday against Bowling Green in the little Ohio town south of Toledo with the name of (you guessed it), Bowling Green.

Tommy hit Mitch Heimlich deep for a 74-yard touchdown pass early in the first quarter. The extra point was good by yours truly.

Mid-way through the second quarter, LT took one off our right guard (not the deodorant), broke three tackles and scampered 36-yards to paydirt. Needless to say, I converted another PAT.

On our first drive of the second-half we went up 21-0. This time Tommy hit Scotty on a little buttonhook that he caught on the ten-yard line and easily danced his way to touchdown-land.

In the fourth quarter, Bo went back to his Woody Hayes roots, handing the ball off to LT ad nauseum. Thus, we did a bunch of punting and gave up two TDs. Their place kicker shanked both of his try's way to the left, like a radical Democrat, and we walked away with a 21-12 win.

I have to admit, in spite of being perfect with my toe all day, all season actually, if you don't count those bad snaps by Squeaky, my mind isn't on football. Baseball has dominated the week. Bill Patterson, a Kansas City Athletics scout showed up on Tuesday at practice, hanging around until Bo cut us loose as dusk turned to dark. Patterson came bearing gifts. Now Patterson isn't Greek, but my father had told me to be beware of him anyway. Sure enough, he drew out of his trunk a heavy box containing a dozen Louisville Slugger baseball bats. He pulled one out and handed it to me. At the top it was perfectly embossed with the words, "Genuine Billy Boyd Model S-2."

"Just a little gift for my favorite college pitcher," Patterson said to me.

I quickly handed the bat back to him with a reminder that it was a violation of NCAA rules for me to accept them.

Patterson came right back at me, stating it would be perfectly fine if I were to drop out of Miami and sign the contract with the Athletics for One-Hundred and Ten Thousand dollars, a copy of which he just happened to have tucked in his suit pocket.

Now that's a shitload of money. I swallowed hard, tried not to pass out, then politely, but firmly, told him that I had committed to my parents that I would finish my senior year and graduate from Miami, before considering any offers to play baseball. I then gave back to him the official *Billy Boyd* bat from Louisville and suggested June 8th would be a good day to talk. Graduation day is June 7th. Patterson grudgingly got the message, climbed into his Ford convertible and headed out of Oxford.

After my shower, I immediately called home to report the Patterson capper. Dad suggested that I should tell both of my coaches, Schembechler and Anderson. Since Bo was down the hall, I started with him. He really impressed me by being both complimentary of how I had handled Patterson while offering some very good sage advise on how to navigate the rest of my senior year. He agreed that what Kansas City was proposing was a wheel barrel full of dollar bills, but it was wise to postpone the big payday for a few more months. He pointed out that the number would only get larger if I had the kind of spring everyone expected.

After dinner I called Andy. His response was similar to Bo's. He did make it very clear that had I not immediately returned the bats, I would have become ineligible to strut my athletic prowess any longer at Miami.

When I explained the little episode to Brooksie later that night at the library, she just smiled and joked that Bags would have kept the bats.

My father was at the game yesterday. One of his best pals is a Bowling Green graduate named Ernie Montgomery. So, Ernie and dad came up together from Cincinnati. Good trip for Dad... bad one for Ernie. Ernie is a very successful attorney who lives in the exclusive Cincinnati neighborhood of Indian Hill.

Last spring, when Ernie was invited to join the prestigious Camargo Country Club, Dad said to him, "Well Ernie, baby, you finally convinced that pack of rich Republicans that you're not Negro, Jewish, Italian, Irish or a Commie and that you have enough scratch in your bank account to afford the initiation fee, as well as the monthly dues, the Friday night seafood buffet and the two-drink minimum. Now if you can just fix that slice."

To his benefit, Ernie turned down that $50,000 opportunity for snob-hood, promising to continue his regular Saturday game at Avon Field Public Links with his best pals, Dad (Irish), Geno Generalli

(Italian) and Sam Katz (Jewish), all old friends from the Withrow High School Class of 1934.

Who said honor and character are dead? Not with good old Ernie!

I should check on Camargo though. Old Bags Brooks might be on the Board.

Actually, it is Lexington Country Club, Horse Town's most exclusive hangout, opened in 1901, where Bags hones his golf game, tells horse stories, smokes $3 cigars and plays skins games for $100 per hole; and where Miss 1940 sips martinis with Lexington Royalty, many of whom spend several days a week there each summer, gossiping and working on their tans and backhands.

Have I mentioned that Nan has a hell of a backhand?

November 10, 1963

Yesterday was Dad's Day at Miami. For the football team, that means before kick-off the players get to parade their fathers out to the fifty-yard line, where the seniors and their fathers are introduced by legendary announcer Charlie Van Outer.

Dad has developed a close friendship with two other fathers. LT's dad, Henry Trimble and his wife Shirley, bonded with my parents early after LT and I hooked up at Woodward. They have played bridge together on the third Saturday of each month for several years now. Henry and Dad have also shared several gallons of Hudepohl, Cincinnati's finest lager and Jamison's, Ireland's finest hair remover, while burning to a crisp a few truckloads of burgers and dogs.

The other member of this three-man *dad-fraternity* is Oliver "Ollie" Biadasz, father of linebacker, Pauly Biadasz. Pauly played his high school ball for a very good Purcell High School team that beat Woodward 48-6 our junior year. Pauly is one mean sumbitch. So, it didn't take LT long to officially dub him *Pauly Badass*!! One suggestion... don't tell any Polish jokes around Pauly.

After the fathers and sons took our collective bows, the dads gathered behind our bench to enjoy the game from the side lines with their sons' names pinned on their backs.

Yesterday was unusually warm for early November. A perfect football day. And the Redskins were almost perfect as well. The jock-dads were treated to a lopsided 40-8 win over the Toledo Rockets. The Rockets never got off the ground. Actually, they crashed and burned. OK, I'll stop with the puns.

All I will say is that Pauly did prove to be a badass, LT ran rampant, scoring four TDs, Tommy threw the ball for over 200 yards, and I kicked seven extra points and one field goal. One unusual statistic is that each team scored a safety. Toledo got theirs on another one of the now famous bad snaps by Squeaky, that was the closest thing to a rocket we saw all day.

The only thing wrong with Dad's Day is that Nan also has a dad. Yep, Bags is back in town, with the beauty queen in tow. I have been avoiding the unavoidable, that being, keeping Mom, Dad and Liz away from the Brooks.

Well last night that came to an end. Bags and Miss 1940 did not disappoint. They were their glorious stuffed-shirt selves. They patronized the holy shit out of Danny and Kayleigh Boyd. But Mom and Dad were up to the task, as was my cheerleading sister. I actually delighted in how both of my parents staved off the constant flow of fluff and bullshit with grace and humor, while Liz looked on with awe. Unfortunately, Nan was mortified for a while. Seeing how Danny Boy and Kayleigh stood their ground, she was able to lighten up. Liz was seated next to Nan and I think they finally became real friends. Liz was amazed that sweet little Brooksie could possibly have been raised by those two, while Nan truly sensed the empathy emanating from my sister.

The event was held on neutral ground, as we had the good sense to arrange dinner at Al and Larry's up town. So, the choices were three-two beer, burgers or grilled cheese. No martinis. No wine lists. No snails. No food set on fire. Just college town fare.

Of course, the predictable came up. What kind of a living did a pharmacist (Dad) make? Why was my mother (and English teacher) working? Had my mother (half Jewish) been to Israel? The Boyds had never been to the Derby... really? Did Liz just love being a cheerleader? And, so on and so forth.

Miss America-third-runner-up constantly referred to my mother as "dear" or "Kay" which is normally verboten. But Mom just went with it, admitting she had no idea who was Miss America in 1940, but was certain that Francis must have been cheated and should have won. She played along with the name game, asking Francis if there might be a connection between Fran and Nan.

Francis Brooks took a second to light a cigarette and replied, "Darling, it is Francis and Nancy," giving me a bullet stare on "Nancy." Clearly, she didn't like that I referred to her daughter as "Nan" or "Brooksie."

Mom came right back with, "Oh, Francis dear, I understand completely. I only answer to Kayleigh. And if it were up to me, we would still call Liz by her real name, which is Eiles, and Billy would still be William. But nicknames are a big deal in our humble little family, right Daniel?"

Francis Brooks may be a fox, but she had no idea she was being out foxed by Kayleigh Boyd. Danny the pharmacist did. And I'm pretty sure Bags did also... and was enjoying it and falling in love with my mother.

As they say, all's well that ends well. A few blows had been landed. But no blood had been drawn. For me, the highlight of the night was the subtle bonding of Liz and Nan. It had only taken 10 months.

NOVember 17, 1963

{{{

I f there can be a hero in a football game that ends in a tie, yesterday was my turn. With three seconds on the clock and the Redskins down to the Dayton Flyers by a score of 27-24, Bo did something that he would normally never do. He put all of his money of me (and Squeaky too).

With the ball sitting on the Dayton 31-yardline, Bo used our last time out and grabbed me by the face mask and said, "Billie, go tie this fucking game."

Then he grabbed Squeaky by his face mask and stated so the whole team and the first ten rows at Memorial stadium could hear, "Number 60, if this snap isn't perfect, they will be burying your fucking ass on Tuesday. Do you read me?"

Out we trotted, Tommy setting up to receive the snap on the 39-yard-line. As it turned out, both Squeaky and I were obedient. My kick was straight and true and we had tied the game at 27-27 as time ran out. The 49-yard field goal set a new Miami record... you are welcome.

On some days a tie is a win. Yesterday was one of those days. We had come back from a 27-7 half-time deficit to catch the Flyers. I was carried off the field in front of Mom, Dad and Mir who had driven up to Dayton for the game. For the first time this year, football had become fun. As LT said to me at the end of the game, "You did it, B-3. Fuck the Wright Brothers!!"

Liz, having cheered her ass off all afternoon, gave me a big hug at mid-field, pointed to where Mom, Dad and Mir were sitting, and we had a silent family moment. This tie felt a whole lot different than the one to Xavier the first week of the season. It's the difference between, "should have won" vs. "should have lost."

Next week is our last game of my college career when we take on Cincinnati at Nippert Stadium. Unlike last year when Johnny Pont took us to the Tangerine Bowl, a post season offer seems out of the question this year.

This past week required a lot of reading for classes and trying to read Brooksie. She hasn't been her fun loving, carefree girlfriend self. Literally, since Homecoming weekend and the Maisonette dinner there has been an edge to her. And the Dad's Day gathering at Al and Larry's last week, watching the contrast between her parents and mine, has certainly compounded her funk. Worse yet, I don't know what to do to help.

I'm hoping that once the football season ends, I will be able to give her more attention.

At any rate, LT and I had originally planned another night at the Dixie Manor Hotel in Hamilton with Jan-Mar and Brooksie. But when Nan met the team bus behind Withrow court last night I immediately knew that was not in the cards.

Nan and I have been cautiously working our way into the sexual

component of our relationship. (I can't believe I just wrote that...
"Component?" Holly shit. Sorry diary). But we have enjoyed being
intimate. Nan is not what LT would call a "headboard grabber and
screamer." But that was never what I was looking for.

I clearly am the more experienced at activities that take place between two people with their clothes off. But Nan was no virgin when
we met. We both know what we are doing. And she prefers "gentle."

My read last night was that a movie, popcorn, hand-holding and a
little late-night petting, was the right call. A second James Bond movie
called "From Russia with Love" is playing at the Western Theater
uptown. When I was a freshman, I read the whole Bond collection
written by a former British spy guy named Ian Fleming. They were
all full of intrigue, gorgeous women who all put out at the drop of a
martini, and impossible feats by the hero, James Bond, while dressed
in a tux. What's not to love.

Bond was just what the doctor ordered. We took a seat in the last
row and watched Bond kick the holy shit out of a dozen bad guys not
to mention Lotte Lenya who had a dagger in the toe of her shoe. Nan
and I just held each other for two hours. Not a word about families
was mentioned which was just what we both needed. I even got to
practice unhooking a bra with one hand.

NOVEMBER 23, 1963

Today I was supposed to be headed to Nippert Stadium on the University of Cincinnati Campus for the final game of this 1963 season. Instead, I am seated in my room in our little suburb of Roselawn forcing myself to write this, because I know I must.

Yesterday afternoon, President John Fitzgerald Kennedy, was shot and killed while riding through downtown Dallas Texas in an open limousine with his wife Jackie seated next to him.

It seems unreal. But I know its real because I saw Jackie Kennedy in her blood-soaked dress last night on NBC. And this morning, Dad and I watched someone roll JFK's famous rocking chair from the White House and onto a moving van while Edmund Newman confirmed that Lyndon Baines Johnson is now the President. The pain and disbelief are unbelievable and unbearable. LT and I were on our way to the Rez to hook up with Brooksie and Jan-Mar when we first heard the news. We had to see Walter Cronkite say it on a TV in the main student lounge, and then three more TV confirmations, before I actually believed it.

Jan-Mar immediately broke down in tears. But Nan just squeezed my hand over and over while remaining silent and stoic.

LT and I were required to be at a team meeting yesterday at 5:00, where Bo advised the team that our game scheduled for today had been postponed. We might play on Thanksgiving, but maybe not. He cut us loose until Monday morning.

I brought Brooksie home with me last night. She slept in my room, and I crashed on the couch. The only thing that helped to ease the sting, was for the two of us to be together. She's in the kitchen now with Mom, Mir and Liz whipping up pancakes, bacon, orange juice and coffee.

My mother is almost inconsolable. She had been so joyfully enthusiastic about the Kennedy presidency. It had filled her with almost three years of pride and optimism for a better America. JFK was the first President from her generation and she loved him.

The beauty queen insisted that Nan come home to Lexington last night, which is understandable. Everybody is frightened and seriously shaken at the moment. But Nan stood her ground telling her mother she wanted to be with me and my sisters. Our Miss Brooks wasn't happy but she capitulated when Bags interceded. Apparently, he understood why his daughter wanted to avoid his wife's drama. And he probably doesn't see this as a major event worthy of grief. I have no doubt that Bags contributed big time to the Nixon campaign. And I also know he currently is in deep political love with Barry Goldwater.

I need to stop now, but will try to get more down on paper later as I know this may be the most significant event of my life. Just one question... who the hell is Lee Harvey Oswald?

November 25, 1963

Today they will bury JFK at Arlington National Cemetery on a hillside plot that looks back across the Potomac River at the Lincoln Memorial. The papers say that Jackie will light an eternal flame... another tear-jerker.

I just couldn't write any more on Saturday or yesterday. This whole thing has gone from tragic to heartbreaking to insane to deranged. And it turns out the weekend has provided not one, but two crazed imbeciles.

Just as we were learning a little something on TV about this guy Lee Harvey Oswald, who they claim shot Kennedy from some building in downtown Dallas, when some other bozo gangster type named Jack Ruby, rubs out Oswald, all right under the nose of the Dallas Police, and on live television. It has been just too much to digest.

Saturday was cold but sunny. Nan and I took a couple of long walks. We were joined on the first one by my two sisters and Mir's boyfriend, Sidney Warren. I really like the kid. He doesn't have an athletic bone in his body. But he is very smart, and also wise beyond his 18 years. Mir seems to have a great connection with him.

Later in the day, I walked Nan the mile and a half up Reading Road to Woodward High School, so she could see the old alma mater. By Saturday afternoon the reality of the assassination was sinking in.

Then yesterday, as a family, we watched Ruby shoot Oswald in the basement of the Dallas Police Station. I mean, really? Right in front of our eyes they kill the suspect. And if that wasn't enough, they moved Kennedy's body from the White House to the US Capitol. So, we now have visions of a horse drawn caisson along with this riderless horse with military boots reversed in the stirrups, while a steady drumbeat, or the strains of Chopin's Funeral March or the Naval Hymn, plays in the background.

We spent most of Sunday gathered in our living room watching this *spectacle*, until it was time to head back to Miami. Mom wanted Liz and me to stay in Cincinnati. But that wasn't in the cards. While our game with Cincinnati was postponed, it is now scheduled for Thanksgiving Day, and Bo expected us back today for more practice.

And Liz preferred to get back to school as well. So, LT collected Brooksie, Liz and me in his beat to shit Ford at 4:30 and off we went.

Nan and I have had some deep conversations in the last two days. Unlike her parents, something in her life has skewed her view on things political and culturally way to the left of the way she was raised. This means she now aligns with me and the rest of the Boyd clan.

But I knew that the first night with her. It was her parents that blew my mind. The last two days have certainly drawn Nan and me closer.

If an event like the assassination of a beloved president is like a deadly infection, LT insists that humor is the greatest antibiotic.

So, given that Cincinnati wouldn't allow senior, Jim Cooley, AKA

Hiawopbop, to ride his horse onto their Nippert Stadium lawn, he will instead be leading us onto the field on Thanksgiving Day, running and screaming like a banshee.

Thus, earlier today, LT pulled all of the seniors on our team together and proclaimed, "OK, boys. No Hiawopbop on horseback on Thursday. That means Jim has ridden his last ride at Miami. And we are going to honor him.

Here's the deal. Most of you nimrods are unaware that the most famous Miami Indian Chief was named *Little Turtle*. Well, that's a bullshit name. So is Hiawopbop. Therefore, by the end of practice each of you are going suggest a better name for Jim when he runs out on the field Thursday. This is non-negotiable because I'm the fucking Chief!!'""

In our locker room after practice, here is what was handed to LT by the brilliant Class of 1964 footballers:

- *Chief Running Bare As*s (in honor of the 1960 Johnny Preston hit)

- *Chief Little White Glove* (also honoring that song)

- *Chief Chasing Your Squaw* (Honoring most of the defensive backfield)

- *Chief Cloud of D*ust (In honor of Bo's play calling)

- *Chief Shitting Bull* (You've all heard of Sitting Bull… no shit)

- *Chief Crazy Horses As*s (Honoring the back side of Cooley's palomino)

- *Chief Wanna See My Teepee* (For the perverts on the team)

- *Chief Schem Bec Liar* (Someone questioning Bo's honesty)

- *Chief Afraid of Bobcats* (Ohio U's win streak against the Skins)

- *Chief Can't Catch Ball* (In recognition of our receivers)

- *Chief Billy Big Toe* (Recognizing yours truly)

- *Chief Pulling Guard* (Honoring our slow-ass guards)

- *Chief Can't Snap Ball* (You guessed it... for Squeaky)

- *Chief Lar-Curl-Moe* (For all of the stooges on the team)

- *Chief Me Smokem Weed* (No comment... but not my submittal)

- *Chief My Pop's No Wop* (No doubt from Pollock Pauly Badass)

- *Chief Cold Cheese* (From some genius who can't spell Cochise)

- *Chief Pilgrim Suck Big One* (We must have a real Indian on the team)

LT's responded to this ludicrous list by stating, "You know what? The 23rd President of the United States, Benjamin Harrison graduated from Miami. The thing I'm most sure of after reading these suggestions is that the second president from Miami is not on this football team. We're sticking with Hiawopbop!!"

Then looking at me he said, trying not to laugh, "Chief Billy Big Toe? Are you shitting me?"

Bottom line, LT has the team laughing again. And JFK is still dead.

December 1, 1963

I have been so pissed off and I just can't get over it. At least the goddamned football season is finished. We polished off UC two days ago in a close one, 21-19. LT scored two of our three touchdowns. I hit all three points-after and now I can move on to baseball and healing.

After the game, Bo came to me in the locker room and thanked me for a great season, showing a warmth I had not seen all year. Reminding me that he had played both football and baseball at Miami, he promised to catch as many games as possible next spring.

Everybody is pretty screwed up. Nan went home for Thanksgiving, partly because her parents insisted, and probably because I've been a total asshole since they buried Kennedy.

As she got into daddy's limo Wednesday afternoon to head back to Lexington, her parting shot after a kiss on the cheek was, "You know Billy Boy, this assassination didn't just happen to you. Call me after you get your shit together."

Lately she has referred to me as *Billy Boy* to signal that she feels I am coloring outside the lines, if you will. And her hint to LT for the same crimes and misdemeanors was to call him *Hot Shot*. And when he shows up with a date other than Jan-Mar, all he hears for the rest of the night from Brooksie is *Hot Shot*.

But here I go again, veering off-subject.

So, after the game on Thursday, the Boyd clan did our best to get down to what is usually our favorite meal of the year. But not so much this year. The ladies in the house made most of the food in advance so they could saunter on down to Nippert Stadium in Clifton to watch me put up the last three points of my college football career. Mom put a twenty-pound turkey in the oven to allow it to cook while the Redskins handed the Bearcats a fourth straight defeat against the Skins. Yep, we went 4-0 against Cincinnati during my years at Miami. But there wasn't much celebration.

My two surviving grandparents, Grandma Bahny and Grandma Ruth joined us, as always. Grandma Ruth, tapping into her Jewish side, wasted no time with the pointed interrogation.

"So, Billy, Bubbe, I hear you're taking up horseback riding. Aren't you a little too big for a jockey?"

"Mother, please," my mom interrupted.

"Have you met Whirlaway or Citation?" Grams persisted.

"Whirlaway is dead, Mother," my mother pushed back with a wry smile.

"Well Citation isn't. Have you met him yet?"

I looked over to Grandma Bahny, who was clearly enjoying the Jewish approach to Thanksgiving conversation, before responding back to my other grandmother, whose contribution to the Thanksgiving fest was her famous Matzo Pudding.

"Grams, Citation lives three farms down from the Brooks Farm. So, no I haven't had the pleasure. But I'm hoping to meet Dan Patch, Trigger, and Silver sometime soon. Did you know that Roy Rogers is Jewish?"

"Very funny, my little Meeskite," said Grams Ruth, as Grams Bahny cut through it all by asking Ruth for her recipe for Matzo Pudding, as she does every year, with no intention to ever buy a box of matzos. But thankfully she had changed the subject. For Bahny Boyd, matzo was just an over-sized dry cracker.

It was good having the older generation of the family at the table. I learn something every time they come around. On this Turkey Day, they both recalled the assassination of James Garfield when they were young girls.

Grams Bahny explained that the real concern her family had was that Teddy Roosevelt was too young and inexperienced to be President.

"Well, you can't say that about Lyndon Johnson," Dad said.

He then followed that with this:

There was a girl from Rabat
Who had triplets, Nat, Pat and Tat;
It was fun in the breeding,
But hell in the feeding,
When she found she had no tit for Tat.

Then, as he often does with Grams Ruth, Dad told a Jewish Grandmother joke. As always, he referred to Grams Ruth as "Safta Ruthie."

"So, Safta Ruthie, a Jewish grandmother is walking on the beach with her grandson. Suddenly a big wave hits the boy and he disappears beneath the water. The grandmother shouts to the sky, 'Dear God I've always been true to you. Please bring back my dear boy.' Another huge wave breaks, depositing her grandson unharmed on the shore. She looks to the sky and exclaims, 'He had a hat.'"

And so it went, as this very unusual Thanksgiving dinner seemed to serve as a valuable healing moment. When we finished, I went to the phone and called Nan long distance (with Dad's permission) and told her I was sorry, knowing I had to fix things before we both returned to Miami. She responded softly with, "I love you, Billy Boy."

I was ready this time. "And I love you more than you know, Brooksie."

And, so, the damage was repaired.

Oh, by the way, the new American Football League held its draft yesterday. The Denver Broncos had called LT, stating they might be interested in him. But they wanted to move him to linebacker.

In perfect LT fashion, without consulting with his parents, he told the Broncos guy that, first, he doesn't ski and he has no interest in backing up any line anywhere, not to mention that, one of his great ambitions in life is to never set foot in Colorado. LT is happily finished with football. You can hang his jockstrap in the Miami Hall of Fame. I love that guy.

December 5, 1963

((

L ast night provided a little, if somewhat embarrassing, diversion from the JFK assassination flu. Bo grabbed LT and me, advising us that we were to attend with him, the Fall Athletic Awards Dinner at Fort Loramie High School, near Sidney Ohio. Like Miami, Fort Loramie teams are known as the *Redskins*.

Why this school, we asked Bo. Simple, he explained. There was a kid named William "Chip" Howard who played quarterback on the football team and pitched on the baseball team. Bo wanted Chip to remain a Redskin for four more years. This was a recruiting trip. To enhance his chances of bringing the Chipper to Oxford in 1964, Bo thought bringing the captains of Miami's football and baseball teams to Fort Loramie would help.So, it was rubber chicken and cold broccoli all around last night. Sadly, Fort Loramie's football team had gone 0-10 this fall. Yet, as we listened to the speeches from the various hayseeds speaking last night, you would have thought that their Redskins hadn't lost a game in 30 years. LT nudged me as we listened to all of the self-denial and nodded at Bo. He was shuffling in his seat with that same look he had when we lost our opener to Xavier. He looked like his head might explode.

When it was Bo's turn at the podium, he wasted no time. His short talk sounded something like this:"Ladies and Gentlemen, I need to tell you that I have never heard such BS in my life. It is no wonder that your team lost every game they played this year. If you continue to congratulate your kids for failure, you better expect them to continue to fail."

As LT and I started to slink down in our chairs, Bo continued by looking down at the Howard kid and said, "Chip, I have seen films of you. You have some raw talent. It's a shame you have had to waste it here. If you can see your way to Oxford, I can promise, you will enter a winning environment. The question you need to ask is can you stand up to the demands of winning? No one will be kissing your ass at Miami."

He then concluded by addressing the Fort Loramie audience, "Folks, we thank you for the cold chicken. It was almost as bad as your football team. I can assure you if you continue to pat each other on the backs and talk about how nice your boys are here in Sidney, you will lose ten more next year. In the meantime, if given the opportunity, I will do my best to turn Chip into a winner. Thank you and good night."

Well, I can tell you there was serious silence in that room. And it was pretty silent on the drive back to Oxford. I will say this; last night will prove to be a major event in building the legend of Bo at Miami. I could see how anxious LT was to tell this story to the gang at Swing Hall.

It was quite a night. LT and I agree that you can expect to see Chip

Howard playing quarterback for the Ohio University Freshman team next year.

December 8, 1963

O n page 73 of a little booklet called the "M-Book" which is handed out each year at America's most beautiful college, there is a dress code. That's right... in 1963 they are telling us how to dress. And, if you look around it would appear that most of the almost 9,600 students are in compliance.

The guidelines include this bullshit as quoted from da book.

"Dress for men should be as simple and neat as it is for women. For fall and spring months, short sleeve shirts in stripes, plaids, solids and especially Madras should be worn."

One guideline that pisses me off is that a sports jacket, a white or blue dress-shirt and a tie are required for dinner when eating at the dorm. With our athletic scholarships, LT and I get three free meals a day. My parents are very fond of most things free, even though I have heard my father often say, "There's no free lunch."

Therefore, something most male students have purchased at Roy

Young's College Shop or Jack's Corner, both uptown on High Steet, are a couple of clip-on ties. These little buggers are already tied with a perfect knot and a hook that clips over a fully buttoned oxford. You won't find them at Shillito's or Rollman's or Pogue's in downtown Cincinnati. No, this is strictly a Joe College item that helps to keep Roy and Jack in business.

But, last night, LT and I decided to forgo the Friday fish. Instead, we opted for something you won't find at the Maisonette or Pigalle's. Taking advantage of the unusually warm early December night we grabbed four wool blankets, collected Nan and Jan-Mar, picked up four cheeseburgers and cokes from the Sangy Man and headed to the sixth fairway of the renowned Miami U golf course. While it was warmer than normal last night, it is December, and we had the entire sixth hole to ourselves.

I think the Sangy Man is unique to Miami. They are a collection of old school buses that have been gutted and outfitted with various cooking capabilities. They sell burgers, dogs, fries, bologna sandwiches on Rubel's rye, various drinks and small cakes and pies, out of a side window. From 7 – 11 each night there is one parked right outside Brooksie's dorm, Well's Hall on Spring Street.

We found a perfect spot to lie down and get caught up on our astronomy. After wolfing down the cheeseburgers, LT got busy fitting Jan-Mar for a new bra, using the tactile method. Nan and I, who had moved a good nine iron away from our respective roommates, held hands, gazed at the stars and talked about the future... well more specifically, our future.

Nan's view of the future is much more in the realm of long-term than mine. She starts on the other side of my prospective baseball career. She already has me signing with the Cardinals, Bags favorite team, using my signing bonus to buy her a ring that Miss 1940 would die for, getting married in the winner's circle at Keenland, getting her daddy a grandson, her mother a granddaughter and helping me write my speech for my induction into the Hall of Fame, which Bags will rent out for a huge celebration, recognizing that the baseball bullshit part of my life is over and I can get down to making some real money like him...WHEW!!

And what's with this fascination that people from Kentucky have with the fucking St. Louis Cardinals? Lexington is less than 100 miles from Cincinnati. Does Bags have something against Frank Robinson? Oh wait... of course he does. But that's a different discussion.

My version of the future is how best to get ready for my senior season next spring and how best to stay clear of Nan's parents as I'm doing so, and not lose Brooksie in the process.

So, as we squeezed each other's hand and tried to find Cassiopeia, I attempted to pull Nan back from her journey to 1984, reminding her of Orwell, so we could discuss the subject in more reasonable terms.

The big question for me is, can Nan possibly be the wife of a guy who makes a living throwing a baseball, hoping to sign for more than sixty-four thousand dollars? That's the question.

Of course, I haven't shared this with Mom, Dad, Mir and Liz. But I have with my pal LT.

His response was, "Whoa!! Put the gun back in the holster, Gunner. You need to make sure you bring the heat again this spring. You need to be registering with the Cincinnati Reds, not Shillito's. You have a whole season yet to play. You can't be spending money you haven't earned yet,"

LT keeps it short and sweet... and on target.

December 18, 1963

I know I haven't registered any gems in this little journal of mine for over a week. So, sue me. I've had a lot on my mind. Brooksie and I have been negotiating the holiday schedule, causing both of us to get a little testy.

We all head out of Oxford tomorrow. The first four days are settled. Brooksie, Jan-Mar, LT and I are all travelling to Cleveland on the famous Miami Christmas train. The chartered four car train will board us at the old Oxford Station at the end of Spring Street, collect 8 smackers from each of us and drop us at the Union Terminal smack in the middle of downtown Cleveland.

The five-hour trip is all party, so we're told. With stops in Dayton, Columbus and Akron, it will be dark by the time we exit in Cleveland.

I was very surprised when Bags and da Queen approved of this little soiree. I think their new strategy is to let Nan get her fill of me so she comes to her senses and marries some plantation owner's son, summers in the south of France, drinks mint juleps and puts out heirs until she croaks from terminal happiness. I'll just play them a game at a time.

Jan-Mar also comes from a fairly wealthy mother and father in Atlanta who divorced, then quickly remarried a half dozen years ago. She is pretty much permitted to play by her own rules. Her parents compete for her affection by giving her anything she wants. But, believe it or not, she doesn't seem spoiled.

Her father is a bigwig with Holiday Inn and secured us two rooms at the famous Cleveland Hotel next to the landmark Cleveland Tower. In theory one room is marked "Boys", the other marked "Girls".

Now, this deal comes with rules from all of the parent people. Yet there will be no parent police to enforce the rules. So, while there will be four beds, two of them may not get much use.

It is becoming more and more apparent that, if there is such a thing, Jan-Mar is LT's kinda gal. She has an extra dose of "cool" with a full shaker of confidence and a double jigger of "I won't be taking any of your bullshit." In other words, she's a female Lenny Trimble.

While Nan and I look at life in terms of years, Jan-Mar and LT seem to view it in days, and in some cases, hours. Long-term planning for them is "what's for breakfast?" and "what sexual position do you want to start with?"

No doubt, that last question will be in play when we get to Cleveland tomorrow night.

On the other hand, my deal with Brooksie has evolved into working through the complexities and realities of actually being in love. It seems that the first big stumbling block is believing that the other person could essentially be in love with you. I guess Nan and I are just trying to honor the process. But that's enough self-analysis.

We are going to Cleveland for some holiday fun. Let the games begin.

December 23, 1963

Only two days until Christmas. And what a mess being in love with a rich girl who lives a hundred miles away can have on the so-called holiday season.

Our trip to Cleveland was fantastic until it wasn't. Along with the free hotel rooms provided by Jan-Mar's dad, he also arranged a Friday night dinner at the Theatrical Grille a few blocks from our hotel. Jan-Mar explained that this was a big deal because it is owned by a famous mobster and was also where Perry Como and Dean Martin got their start in show biz. Plus, it has the best food in Cleveland.

Wait, I've got more. A mysterious fire burned the place down a few of years ago. The new, improved replacement was recently opened by a Cleveland mobster named "Mushy Wexler." Believe it or not, Brooksie knew all about Wexler, as he owns a huge horse farm in Lexington that includes a horse that finished second in the Kentucky Derby, then won the Preakness. Old Mushy and Bags are drinking buddies. I

might have guessed. Just another example of me asking myself just
what the hell I am doing in the middle of all this unwarranted wealth.

So, in addition to the fine food, the place had a big bar and stage
which has featured names like Sinatra, Bennett and the McGuire Sisters, over the years. On the holiday season night that we were part of
the well-healed crowd, it was Louis Prima who was appearing. Now
that would have been great if Keely Smith was part of the act. But she
divorced his Italian ass a couple of years ago. So, it was, as LT put it,
WOP City, with Louis and his famous sax player Sam Butera... rooty
toot toot.

All in all, it was a great evening thanks to Jan-Mar's daddy's Diner's
Club Card. My parents have two credit cards. One for Shillito's
Department store and one for Rollman's, the department store in the
Swifton Shopping Center near our home in Roselawn.

At Dad's Drug Store, credit is extended with a handshake and a
large dose of trust. But Dad isn't in the horse racing business.

As I said, our weekend in Cleveland was Jim dandy until it went
south. That happened on Saturday as Brooksie, Jan-Mar, LT and
I strolled through Halle's Department store. I knew the store and
its reputation for higher end things, because the owner's daughter,
Barbara Halle lives down the hall from Brooksie and Jan-Mar at Wells
Hall.

This is where an unfortunate coincident happened. Who the hell
do we bump into but my ex... Toni Jansen. It hadn't really entered
my mind, but Toni is from Shaker Heights, an upscale Cleveland
neighborhood. Toni was with her mother who politely said, "Well,
hello Billy. What brings you to Cleveland?"

Every time I see Toni, I feel like a heel. Now, here I faced not only
her, but also, her perfectly sweet mother. After stuttering for several
seconds, I introduced Nan and Jan to Toni and her mother and gave a

very vague answer to her question. Of course, Toni knows LT all too well. Nan, Jan and Toni kibbitzed for a while like they were sorority sisters. In the mean-time, LT entertained himself watching me sweat bullets. Thankfully, everyone wished everyone Merry Christmas and we watched Toni and Mrs. Jansen disappear up the escalator in the center of Halle's vast and magnificent first floor.

But later, on Saturday, Nan had a million questions. We had avoided this subject since she first asked me if I loved Toni ten months earlier as we sat at Tuffy's. Nan didn't seem jealous. But she was way too damned curious. This made me tense. Before we both knew it, we were pissed at each other and hotel sex had taken the elevator to nowhere.

Yesterday things had calmed some and the four of us took the New York Central morning train back to Cincinnati, where Dad picked LT and me up, while Brooksie was met by Jerome and the family stretch Lincoln for the drive to Lexington. Jan-Mar took a cab to the airport for her flight back to Atlanta.

Nan and I negotiated our holiday split with a healthy kiss having pretty much put Toni, and all that she implied, to bed, no pun intended. Against my better judgement, I'm headed to Lexington with LT on Friday the 27th. Jan-Mar will be coming up from Atlanta. The Brooks Farm has plenty of bedrooms. Unlike Cleveland, all four of us will be sleeping solo. I suppose nothing will be stirring... not even a mouse.

December 25, 1963

))

M erry Christmas, diary. It's me... Billy McScrooge Boyd.

One of the things I love most about Christmas is how much my Jewish grandmother Ruth loves Christmas. She will have nothing to do with Hannukah. It's almost as if she was raised Catholic.

Now, there is one exception. She always makes Hannukah treats for Christmas. She calls them "cookies from the original", meaning Jesus was a Jew. This is to the delight of the entire Boyd clan; especially my father, who was raised a Catholic, but you'd never know it.

For years we have had our family celebration on Christmas Eve. Grams Ruthie brings three trays of goodies... one each of, what she refers to, as her "three wise cookies."

They include her Hamantaschen, Rugelach, and Dad's favorite, Sufganiyot, which is more like a filled donut than a cookie. As Grams explained to us long ago, the triangular filled Hamantaschen are actually traditionally for the Jewish holiday Purim, (whatever the hell that is). But apparently it has become a Hannukah treat as well. She makes two types; one with a poppyseed filling and the other with one of her homemade jams. I could eat those little treasures by the dozens.

None of us particularly care for the Rugelach. They are basically a filled tiny croissant that are too doughy and flavorless. Yet, they have meaning to Grams mostly because our grandfather Paddy loved them. But the star of the show and clear winner is the Sufganiyot, a round jelly doughnut that is deep-fried, injected with jam or custard, and then topped with powdered sugar. Grams could open a bakery with those snow-covered globes of Christmas gluttony.

At any rate when Mir and I picked Grams Ruthie up last night we had to make two trips in order to get all of her treats to the car.

On the full-bred Irish side of the family, Gramma Bahny gave up on the soda biscuits and sugar biscuits long ago (the Irish refer to cookies as biscuits and apparently never heard of Aunt Jemima or Bisquick). They just can't compete with the Yenta baked stuff. Instead, her contribution is her famous Irish apple pie with a lattice crust. It's all about the Granny Smith apples (readily available in Ohio each fall) and an unbelievably flaky crust.

Mom, not to be denied, provides the Christmas Eve dinner centerpiece, or what the Brooks family would call the piece de résistance. She works some magic on a bone-in ham that is to die for. And guess who is the biggest fan? You got it... our Jewish Grandmother Ruthie Shulman Broderick. She started chomping on pork with the first BLT gramps Paddy bought for her at the Dow Drugs lunch counter, as the story goes, and she has never looked back.

So, while the Yiddish recipes survive, the restrictive Kosher diet was swept away by love.

Frankly, last night proved to be a great Christmas Eve and just what we all needed. Ruthie and Bahny kept us in stitches with tales of days long gone. Dad consumed enough Jameson's to try to sneak in several of his more bawdry limericks including:

There once was a young man from Lyme Who married three wives at a time. When asked, "Why a third? He replied, "One's absurd, And, bigamy, sir, is a crime!

And the one that got him a smack to the back of the head:

There once was a young man named Fritz Who planted a field full of tits, They came up in the fall Juicy nipples and all And he cheerfully chewed them to bits

Of course, when Grams Ruthie and I both laughed at that beaut, Liz cracked my skull and Mom, addressing her mom said, "Mother, please don't encourage them."

Grams Bahny just accused Dad of being just like his father (her deceased husband) and Dad reminded her that she was the one who married him.

After all of that, gifts were passed out to the pleasure of all of the family. It seemed to me that a little more thought went into the gift-giving this year. Perhaps it is the Kennedy factor.

This morning as I write this, Mom, Liz and Mir are in the kitchen coaxing along Mom's eggs, sausage, bacon, beans, mushrooms, diced potatoes and tomatoes mess. When you're Irish, you have to eat some weird shit... even on Christmas morning. But we've been scarfing down this crap all of our lives. Pass the soda bread.

We got a bunch of snow overnight, so dad is pridefully constructing the perfect fire in our living room fireplace, in his constant quest to turn the Boyd home into a Currier and Ives print. Nobody can build a fire like Dad... just ask him. Quick, somebody find a camera.

Later on, Christmas Day

Well, I thought I was finished reporting on Christmas 1963. But I just hung up from Brooksie. First, let me just say "Holy Shit." Man, I don't want to be rich. Second, let me report the crazy news. Her Christmas gift from her looney tune parents was a brand spanking new Porsche 356-B Cabriolet Ruby Red Roadster (convertible) with black rag top and tan interior. Wait before I go on, I need to let that sink in.A FUCKING PORSCHE?

But this is the Brooks family, so, of course, it gets better. Miss Kentucky Bourbon 1940 apparently needed a bigger boat. So, you will find floating at their private pier on Lake Cumberland this spring, something called a Hatteras Double Cabin Motoryacht. I should have known she could never be satisfied with their 25-foot Chris Craft ski boat. This new floater, according to Brooksie, is 41 feet long and sleeps 10 people. Bags had the thing sitting by the main horse barn this morning sporting a huge red ribbon, being towed by a semi-truck and parked next to the Porsche (ribbon also included).

This may be hard to believe, but it gets better yet. After touring the yacht and the 356-B, Bags dragged Our Miss Brooks and Nan over to his private hanger at the Lexington Airport where his company keeps a Grumman Gulfstream 1 twin engine turboprop, because flying first class on Piedmont or Delta isn't good enough. He bought the company plane in 1961. It seats 12, has a galley, bar and small desk, and he is proud that he got it for a steal of just over a half mil. Sitting next to the Gulfstream this morning, was Bags' gift to himself, a Cessna 310 four-seater. Brooksie advised me that Bags is taking flying lessons and will be in the left front seat pulling back on the stick by Easter.

My reaction was to ask Nan how Santa got all of that shit into his sleigh. To be fair, I could smell the embarrassment coming through the phone line as she unenthusiastically described all of the above in a measured and nervous manner. After a long pause I ask Nan if I could take a spin in the Porsche? Then I said, "Well, what the hell Nan, he sells airplane parts. What took him so long?"

She laughed that adorable little giggle that I love. Then she asked what I got for Christmas. After falsely depicting the Rocket Ship from Mom and Dad, I fest up and described the reality of receiving a couple of 16 ½-34 oxfords, a real paisley tie that I will have to tie myself, and tickets to a Saturday night Cincinnati Royals basketball game in January.

Then I told her about the big bone we got for Crosby our Irish Setter. Yeah, we have a dog. Crosby is a gorgeous creature. Watching him run is a beautiful thing. But he is dumber than a head of cabbage. Dad named him for his favorite singer, the old crooner, Bing Crosby. He spends most of his life next to Dad's chair in the living room. The only two things the Irish Monster (my name for him) does well is shed and shit. Make that three things. He loves to eat too, which is why he shits mountains every day. We love him anyway.

Enough about Christmas. I'm going to take the Irish Monster for a walk.

January 3, 1964

{{{

Happy New Year y'all (as they say in Lexington). Well, the New Year is here and LT and I are back on campus. And the Chicago Bears beat the New York Giants a few days ago at Wrigley Field which is a fucking baseball field. George Halas is King of Football again.

Classes resume on Monday and we are in the final stretch of College Joe life. For LT it will be funny and fun. For yours truly? Well, it could be really great. Then there's always the possibility it might be a shit storm. Baseball is still too far off. And the expectations are too high.

I want this whole thing to start tomorrow. But practice won't begin for two months and our first game, against Xavier, is almost three months off.

There is an Irish proverb that goes, "A friend's eye is a good mirror."

I spend a lot of time with LT. And he is good at looking a person

right in the eye. At the moment, his stare is telling me that I need
to cool it. I am spacing out over the pressure of the anticipation
of the upcoming baseball season. But also, LT clearly sees that my
real conundrum is my affection for Brooksie banging up against my
discomfort with the decadent wealth and snobbery of her parents.
The truth that LT understands is that I want her more than anything
ever. But I want her to be from a little Cape Cod home like ours in
Roselawn, not some giddy up horse farm in Lexington. Well too bad
Billy, says LT's eyes.

Last Friday LT and I hopped into his banged-up jalopy and headed
the two hours south on US 27 to Lexington. When we arrived, we
were greeted by Jackson, the butler. I know. I know. Just more wealth
in your face.

Jackson is a very cool negro cat, who really digs baseball. We immediately hit it off on my two summer visits to Brooks Ridge Farm.
And sadly, the Brooks predictably have one of those little statues of a
very black guy dressed as a jockey holding a black chain ring, sitting
in their 3-acre front yard just to remind Jackson he's not far removed
from slavery, so they will treat him as such.

Jackson politely grabbed our bags and showed us to our palatial
rooms that sat next to each other on the second floor of the Brooks
mansion. Brooksie showed up as we were unpacking and hurried us
down to the heated sunroom surrounded by floor to ceiling windows,
where a large table was set for lunch. Our view was acres of rolling
bluegrass, miles of white fencing and a half dozen thoroughbreds
prancing about. They are probably worth more than my parents have
made in their lifetime.

But, as LT said to me on the drive down, "B-3, shut the fuck
up about the senior Brooks, and focus on Nan and let's have some
fucking fun. Do you think she'll let me take Jan-Mar for a spin in the

Porsche?"

His hardy laugh said he really didn't give a shit about the Porsche, but he was looking forward to getting under Jan-Mar's hood.

While we were trying to figure out where and when to take a seat, the very same Jan-Mar appeared with Brooksie's mom, both sporting bloody Mary's with a huge stalk of celery blooming from the blood.

Our Miss Brooks cheerfully said, "Boys, what can we get you to drink?"

LT opted for a Pabst Blue Ribbon (no glass please, which seemed to displease the house matriarch) and I down-graded to and an ice tea, which made her eye me suspiciously.

As soon as Mumsie had assigned seats, Bags showed up sporting a Kentucky bourbon with a Texas-sized ice cube in an Old Fashion glass.

He advised us all that we had to get down to business on the lunch deal because he had a surprise for Francis Brooks.

He gleefully announced, "Now y'all listen up, ya hear. Old Larry Brooks is takin' his bride, Francis Middleton Brooks down dare to da Fontainebleau Hotel in Miami Beach where we will be celebratin' New Years and attendin' that there Orange Bowl game ta watch dem Cornhuskas from Nebraska take on dem der Tigers from Auburn to see who has the biggest cajones, on New Year's Day. Now ain't that something? 1964, here comes da Brooks."

"But you just wait there, Darlin' Francis... there's more. On New Year's Eve we are headed to the La Ronde Room at the Fontainebleau for the Judy Garland dinner show. How 'bout them apples, Peaches?"

After Peaches finished swooning, he followed up with, "Now then... here's the rules while we're gone. Billy, you and ole LT there will be staying on the west wing of da second floor and are not to go east of da main staircase, ya hear?"

"And Sugar," he said addressing Nan, "You and that pretty little

Georgia Peach over there (Jan-Mar) are sentenced to staying in the east wing... Get my drift?"

"Now y'all can just go ahead and knock yourselves out here on the first floor. Play all the bumper pool y'all want. Just stay outta my office and don't be drinking any of the expensive wine. And if you do drink, y'all stay put right here at Brooks Ridge Farm. Dems da rules. No drinking and driving," he concluded.

LT and I had been seated across from each other and took a quick look at one another. LT's eyes were saying, "Get your bags, Bags, and we'll drive you to the airport."

The beauty queen, after catching her breath said, "Well, my goodness Larry. Ya sure know how to treat a lady. I better gobble down this chicken salad and skedaddle upstairs and pack. What time is our flight?"

I glanced at Jan-Mar who was sporting a shit-eating grin. Then I took a long gander at Brooksie. Her smile was eating shit also.

Bags announcement had completely changed my outlook on what was left of 1963.

Long story short, the despicable Brooks disappeared to the tropics and the rest of us were thrilled to hibernate in the warmth of the Brooks Mansion for a few days. Nobody picked up a cue stick, but we cued up some serious love making as there was all kinds of violations of the demilitarized zone (the main stairs). The only time we left the house (if you can call a mansion a house) was to have an early New Year's Eve dinner at the Columbia Steak House, where the owner knew Nan. Thus, our dinners were paid for with a simple signature by Brooksie (unfucking believable). Thanks Bags.

As it turned out, the Brooks had provided Nan and me exactly what we needed... some serious alone time. Time to run the table on love-making and time to talk about our future. And she gave me the most memorable New Year's I could have hoped for.

By the time LT and I left to return to Cincinnati yesterday, Nan had convinced me that if she could have a life with me, she didn't care if she drove that Porsche another mile and would be happy to never ever shop again for a Derby Fascinator (that's what those lopsided Kentucky Derby hats are called, I just learned). She was ready to go wherever baseball might take us, except St. Louis... fuck Bags and his cock-a-doodle Cardinals. I believe we are engaged to be engaged.

To continue our celebration of the new year, LT suggested that we stop at Biancke's Restaurant in Cynthiana on the way home. They are famous for their family style home cooking. For some reason this little restaurant is often called the Halfway House, which really pisses off LT.

When we entered, he gave me a little shove and said, "Halfway House my ass, B-3. This place is the Two-Thirds House if you're from Cincinnati and the One-Third House if you're from Lexington. Why can't these fucking Hillbillies get anything right. They have damned good chicken, but they suck at math.

"What do you say to that? I chose zero and we sat down with a passel of hillbillies and ordered the fried chicken. For a buck and a quarter, that comes with mashed potatoes, string beans, creamed corn, slaw (Cole or hot), great biscuits and some raucous gravy that LT slathers on everything but his Cole slaw. He polished off lunch with one of Biancke's renowned root beer floats.

When we left LT tossed me the keys and said, "B-3, I'm too fat to drive at the moment. Let's get our asses back to good old MU baby, and get on with fucking 1964 y'all!!!"

1964 indeed. When I entered Miami back in the fall of 1960, this year seemed so far off. I looked forward to a little football, a little baseball, a little nookie, and good enough grades to get me into law school somewhere.

The time has flashed by, and now I'm in love with just about the best-looking piece of womanhood I could hope to find. And, I have also become one of the most sought-after athletes in America's class of '64. Yep, that's a lot more than I bargained for back in 1960. Well, as LT often says, "Pass me another Trojan 3-pack and bring it on!"

January 26, 1964

It has been more than three weeks since I have penned an entry in my little leather-bound journal/diary. The two main reasons for this lull have been Brooksie and studying for final exams. And a third reason, I guess, is that over the Christmas break, I took time to read what I have written so far. Thus, I asked myself if I have been too self-absorbed and, more importantly, have I offered too many personal details about Nan and her parents? So, I've been contemplating all of this.

On the later subject I have decided that if I'm going to do this little review of my senior year, I need to tell it like it is. Honesty is the best policy. So, while we all know that too much honesty can be way too much for some people to bear, I have decided to forge ahead.

However, I have also realized that registering all of these truths have added to my neurosis over the upcoming baseball season as well as my ongoing falling in love escapade. On most days I am far more consumed with Nan than anything else. But taking my little writing hiatus has helped to clear my brain. I studied hard and long and feel I nailed my exams, which ended yesterday. Last Saturday, LT and I used my Christmas tickets to watch the Royals beat the St. Louis Hawks by a score of 121-120 in a fantastic game, with Oscar Robertson putting up 40 points, while my man, former Miami star Wayne Embry, added 26 points. It was a great distraction.

I should note that I have also focused on Brooksie. Instead of avoiding the issue, we have spent the last few weeks discussing both of our feelings about how a middle-class baseball phenom from modest means can make it work with a wealthy sophisticate that is intensely intelligent and incredibly gorgeous (which, of course, she dismisses). No tap dancing around the reality... no bullshit. Just honest dialogue. To paraphrase Ramses II from The Ten Commandments, so it is done, so it shall be written.

As it turns out, Nan has convinced me that she would likely have enjoyed a much happier youth had she grown up like me and my sisters, rather than in the isolation of Brooks Ridge Farm and being educated at Sayre School, arguably the best private school in Kentucky.

The bottom line is that I really have no regrets about how I was raised and, while Nan insists that she loves her parents, she would have preferred a much more modest environment for her youth. What I can't figure out is how she has wound up so grounded and seemingly happy, considering her upbringing. Thankfully I have LT to remind me, "Shut up B-3, and just bless your fucking lucky stars."

After a little reflection, I'm going with that. Thank you, Stars of Luck.

So, anyway, I do have one interesting thing to report. To his benefit, Coach Andy Anderson has admitted to me that he has pretty much reached his limit in teaching me anything more about pitching. So, yesterday, he introduced me to Cincinnati Reds pitcher, Joe Nuxhall. Nuxhall is known around here as Hamilton Joe, which is really a bit of a misnomer, as he is actually from Fairfield which is just south of Hamilton.

The first thing he said to me yesterday was, "Hey Billy, it is great to meet you. You can call me Nux."

My new friend Nux, wants to get into broadcasting once he can't get the other side out any longer. Thus, he has talked his way into broadcasting Miami basketball games this season, until he has to head south in February for Spring Training.

The other thing that's really neat about Hamilton Joe is that he holds the distinction of being the youngest person to ever play in the major leagues. At the wee age of 15, Nuxhall pitched against the Cardinals in June of 1944. This was due in large part to the depleted rosters because so many big leaguers were fighting in the War. It took another eight years before he again appeared in the majors, but he holds the record.

The main reason Andy wanted me to meet Nuxhall, was to have him help me develop a slider to go along with my fastball, curveball and knuckleball. Over hamburgers at Al and Larry's uptown, my pal Nux, who just happened to have a new baseball with him, conveyed the "art of the slider." Andy had already explained the difference between the grip for the fastball and the curve. As it turns out, Nux suggested that to throw a good slider I should start with my fastball grip. The difference is something he called "wrist supination" or how you cock your wrist before delivery.

Nuxhall invited me to meet him at the Hamilton High gym this week to toss a few and work on my supination. You don't say no to that. So, tomorrow I'm headed fifteen miles south, hoping Nuxhall can add a few shekels to my anticipated bonus.

I chatted with him again last night at halftime of the game between the Skins and Kent State. We blew Kent out of Withrow Court by the lopsided score of 81-44, with Jeff Gehring and Charlie Coles both putting up 19 points and giving Nuxhall a lot to describe in his easy down-home fashion. Also of interest, Toni's new boy pal, Skip Bolden, only scored 7 points, not that I'm really paying attention.

It has been a good week. The Winter Olympics started in Innsbruck, Austria today. Nan and I are on solid footing. I have finished my exams. I have learned a new word (supination) and I have made friends with a major league pitcher. Shabby, this week was not. Can the U.S. win another Gold in Hockey? Not likely.

February 4, 1964

Second semester classes begin tomorrow. I hope it goes as well as the first. Final grades showed up in the mail yesterday. I wound up with one B and the rest As, or a 3.8 GPA, as they say. Per usual, my sister Liz nailed another perfect 4.0, as did that Kentucky chick that I am dating. Liz is a year and a half into her tenure at Miami and has yet to make anything but straight As. She's always been a show-off.

Most of the women on campus would consider that the level of beauty and intelligence to be found in Brooksie is just not fair. But it's just fine with me.

My session with Joe Nuxhall went very well. He is a really down-to-earth guy. That style seems to be serving him well as a broadcaster of MU Basketball. If you've seen that Dizzy Dean movie "The Pride of St. Louis" starring Dan Dailey, then you might have a feel for how Nux calls a game.

This same "ah shucks" approach proved to make him great for

teaching me how to throw a slider. He had me supinating my ass off by the end of our session in Hamilton last week. Since then, I've been throwing with LT at Withrow Court every afternoon. I am confident that the slider is now part of my pitching repertoire.

The NCAA rules are kind of interesting. I can go over to Withrow Court or out to the athletic fields and throw a baseball all day long with LT... as long as there is not a coach in site. I can even do so with a big-league pitcher such as Joe Nuxhall and not be in violation of the rules. Crazy but true.

As I said, Nuxhall has proven to be a great help to me. He insisted that I take it slow... to treat my arm like it was a family treasure. The Red's left-hander heads to Florida at the end of the month. This is a leap year and the Reds get started in Tampa on the 29th. Joe has promised to work with me one more time before he heads south.

Nux pointed out to me that there is already a handful of Cincinnati-bred players in the majors this year. They include Joe's teammate and last year's Rookie of the Year, Pete Rose, plus Tiger Pitcher, Bill Faul, Phillies pitcher, Art Mahaffey and Senators shortstop, Eddie Brinkman. Nux thinks I could be next. As Grams Ruthie would say, "From his mouth to God's ears." We shall see.

One more thing about Nuxhall; He's a baseball encyclopedia. When we spoke yesterday, he gave me the run-down on the new group just elected to the Baseball Hall of Fame, including a pitcher named Burleigh Grimes, another cat named Heinie Manish and the great Yankees manager, Miller Huggins. I've heard of Grimes and Huggins. Manish? I haven't a clue. But Nux says he had a lifetime batting average of .330. Holly shit Heinie!

After exams, Brooksie shuffled on back to the Farm at Brooks Ridge to visit her favorite colt, Dagmar, the red Porsche, the yellow Cessna, the gray Motoryacht and her very white parents (in that order, I suspect). She calls me each evening, after my dinner and before hers, because she's rich and I'm not. She will be back on campus later today, bringing that luscious body with her. I stand ready.

February 10, 1964

W ell, semester number two of my senior year is under way. I'm finally taking only courses I want to take. All the required shit is behind me. And as much as I love Nan, I have to admit that I am glad she is not in any of my classes this time around. Less pressure always means better results.

Predictably she returned to campus with another news scoop from Lexington. It turns out that some presumed nag that Bags bought for a song last year can run like the wind and has qualified for the Flamingo Stakes in Miami next month. So, of course Bags is having wet dreams that the colt, he has named Lucky Larry, will win in Florida and will be running in the Derby before you can say giddy up.

I hate to admit it. But I'm hoping the Nut's chestnut turns out to be Loser Larry. Shame on me... but I am committed to honesty.

Speaking of honesty, what the fuck is up with this Beatle shit. The four guys with hair like Lucky Larry's mane, were on Ed Sullivan last night singing their hits "All My Loving", "She Loves You", "I Saw Her Standing There" and finally, their first hit, "I Want to Hold Your Hand".

I will admit they have provided the perfect antibiotic to the Kennedy assassination. Their songs are fun and as the saying goes, "easy to dance to." But, Jesus, Mary and Joseph, they're not Elvis.

None-the-less there was a big crowd gathered in front of the TV at Wells Hall last night to catch all of the action. All of the crewcut jocks just stood dumbfounded watching otherwise level-headed coeds swoon through the whole mess. I told Brooksie not to expect me to be going without my regular haircuts... yeah, yeah, yeah!!

I will say this... that Ringo cat is a hoot. Jan-Mar advised LT she will be leaving for Liverpool soon in determined pursuit of George Harrison. She's done with jocks. She wants George. As we like to say in the pitching business, Jan-Mar served up a little "chin music" to old LT last night. He took the "knock-down pitch" and bounced right back up, offering to drive her to the airport, predicting she would likely end up with some smelly old dockworker while George would marry Miss Kentucky 1968 and move with her to the South of France. Brooksie didn't laugh.

One other side note. The Winter Olympics have ended. The USA didn't do for shit. One Gold Metal by some speed skater that nobody has ever heard of. The Commies ran away with the medals. It seems you need five Ks in your name and it has to end in a vowel in order to win a medal.

February 17, 1964

L ast Friday was Valentine's Day. That becomes a big deal when you are in the middle of a serious romance.

Good old Jan-Mar never ceases to amaze the other three of our developing quartet. She concocted a story about a girls' trip to Cincinnati and somehow her hotel daddy scored two rooms at the Sheraton Gibson Hotel just off of Fountain Square in Cincinnati. For a big-time business executive her old man is pretty damned gullible.

Brooksie had little trouble selling the same story to Bags and Queenie primarily because they are preparing for their trip to Miami and arranging travel for Lucky Larry. When it comes to Nan, they often take their eye off the ball. Brooksie joked that Bags told her mom if she was expecting roses for Valentine's, she would have to wait for the Derby in May. Fat chance.

Our biggest problem actually was my sister Liz. But she gets it. I just leveled with her about our plans and her response was a wry grin and a warning that this was going to cost me. My sis really has her shit together.

The weekend proved to be a much better version of our December visit to Cleveland. Our two very wealthy girlfriends, after some serious begging, convinced LT and me to allow them to treat us to dinner at the renowned Maisonette located in the Fountain Square Building on Walnut Street. Again, it was Jan-Mar's father pulling the strings for his happily spoiled daughter and getting us an ungetable reservation for one of the most popular nights of the year. Better yet, the place has a few little private half-moon booths which offer a good deal of privacy. So, of course we had one of those.

I, having been there with Nan and her parents last fall, was eyeing the sole again. But Brooksie suggested the Beef Wellington and it was out of this world. This was LT's first visit and he was happy to let Jan-Mar go for the works. So, it was the Caesar Salad dance, and a bunch of food on fire for them. It is hard to impress LT. But this was a new experience to the nth degree for him. I will say this. He adapted quickly with a little help from his Atlanta belle.

What LT did not see coming was the ultimatum that came at the end of the evening. As he explained to me Saturday morning, in the hotel lobby, Jan-Mar had finally laid down the law. In no uncertain terms, she warned that she was through with our All-Conference footballer, unless he made a full commitment that he was finished trying to fuck his way through the Miami cheerleaders, majorettes and the pom-pom squads. (Of course, he agreed long ago that two of the cheerleaders, Liz and Toni, were exempt).

LT said to me with a wry smile, "B-3, I only needed two more majorettes and a handful of pom-poms. But what the fuck? I haven't found anyone who comes close to Janet Marney (using her full name for the first time in a long while). I guess it is official. I finally have me a girlfriend."

Other than the distraction of a very attractive lady across the dining room loudly panicking over spilling béchamel sauce on her Pierre Cardin cocktail dress, which attracted three waiters, the maître d, and a sous-chef with soda water coming out of their ears, our dinner was pretty nice for a couple of low-class jocks.

It would be indelicate to record how many times Brooksie and I made love over the two nights at the Gibson, but allow me to note it was between 2 and my number on the football team.

On Saturday night, LT and I had sprung for tickets to see the Lerner and Lowe musical, Camelot at the Taft Theater. This play was JFK's favorite. The tickets set us back a pretty penny. But we were with two girls that thought pennies were obsolete.

After the dinner at the Maisonette, and because the eight o'clock show didn't allow for a proper dinner, we had a big lunch at the Temple Deli. Temple's is across the street from Shillito's, Cincinnati's finest department store on 7th Street.

So, unlike rich girls with connections at fancy French restaurants on Friday, I was the one with the Deli connections...pass the corned beef. My mother went to school with Marty Schlecter, son of Moishe Schlecter, the owner of the Temple. Thus, I knew him and got a big welcome from Marty, who was always at the cash register, when the four of us strolled in.

Everyone gagged when I ordered a tongue sandwich on rye. The ladies failed the deli test and ordered turkey sandwiches on white bread. What the hell? They eat all that French shit and won't try corned beef. LT had a Reuben, and he and I added some matzo ball soup. But enough about cuisine.

After lunch we sashayed across the street to Shillito's. Brooksie and Jan-Mar headed for ladies' shoes smack in the center of the first floor, while LT and I chose to take the escalator up to the mezzanine where a large sporting goods offering resided. Two hours later the ladies handed us guys four shopping bags each, to fill our empty hands.

Camelot was very good. They have started to refer to the Kennedy Administration as Camelot. It has been reported that JFK would often listen to the sound track after dinner at the White House. Brooksie loved the show. While she softly sang the words of If Ever I Should Leave You into my ear, Jan-Mar kept LT awake by nibbling on his ear. You might have guessed; Nan has a great singing voice. How do you spell PERFECTION?

The one thing LT and I did agree on, was that even with the free rooms and Friday's dinner, we had blown through a shitload of money. Dating rich girls isn't cheap.

February 25, 1964

I t is late, but I have to get down on paper tonight's news. LT arranged a little football VIP Prize Fight Party to listen to the Cassius Clay – Sonny Liston fight. To assure he and I had no clean-up to deal with, he convinced Squeaky and Badass to hold the event in their large corner room on the second floor of Swing Hall.

To make things more interesting, LT arranged a little betting pool. For a buck you could pick a piece of paper out of one of Squeaky's smelly ballcaps. The papers were marked with a C for Clay and a L for Liston with a number 1-15, representing the round in which the fight would be won. So, there was 30 slips of paper.

The first problem for LT was that there were only 11 of us in attendance, so he had to go into sales mode to get some of the nitwits to buy more than one slip of paper. The second problem was that LT was charging an attendance fee of one dollar each, to cover snacks and drinks.

College jocks are notoriously broke. Thus, five minutes before the fight there was still four slips in Squeaky's chapeau.

LT looked at me and said, "OK B-3, you and I need to pony up another two bucks each to cover the pot."

I was still reeling from our Valentine's sojourn to Cincinnati, and advised LT he needed to find another sucker.

He looked at me like only he can and stated, "Jesus fucking Christ B-3, you're going to be richer than old Larry Brooks in five years and you will own a horse named *Fastball* that will kick old Money Bags nag named *Float My Boat* in the Derby by twenty lengths. Reach in your Kaki pocket and pull out a lousy two Washingtons."

Reluctantly, I handed over the scratch. Looking at the three slips of paper I had drawn, I knew immediately that I was screwed. They all contained a *C* for Clay. Everybody knew Liston was going to kill the Louisville Lip. The only question was in which round Clay would die. Everybody in the room wanted to know who had Liston in the first round, expecting the murder to happen early. Predictably it was LT. It looked like the fix was in. But I knew better. Of the many things you could call LT, cheater was not one of them.

With Badass' radio turned way up, that goofy asshole Howard Cosell introduced Les Keiter, who would call the fight. Clay survived the first round. Then the second.

We listened to round three, hearing that Clay had moved in for a combination of punches and that he had cut Liston near his left eye. Then Les Keiter screamed, "We may be seeing the upset of the century," as we listened in disbelief.

We all crammed closer to the radio. In between the 4th and 5th rounds, we heard Howard Cosell yelling, "Something is the matter with Cassius Clay. He is having trouble with his eyes."

Then the bell rang to start the round, and Keiter said, "One of his trainers says there was something on Liston's gloves, Clay is blinking, says he can't see."

Somehow Clay survived the round. In the sixth round Keiter said, "It's all Clay at the moment."

As the seventh round was beginning to start, we heard Cosell in his distinctive New York accent exclaim, "This is hard to figure out as we come up to round 7. Wait a minute. Wait a minute. Sonny Liston is not coming out! Sonny Liston is not coming out! He's out! The winner and the new heavyweight champion of the world is Cassius Clay! Les, I'm going up into the ring!"

Then suddenly we heard Clay ranting, "I am the greatest. I am the greatest. I am the king of the world. I have upset the world. I told you if you want to go to heaven, I'll get him in 7. I am the king. I am the king."

I quickly scanned the three little pieces of paper in my hand. The second one was marked C-7. Son-of a-buck if I hadn't just won thirty smackers. Yesiree. The Louisville Lip was the GREATEST, and I was thirty bucks richer.

March 2, 1964

We are into March and practice begins in two weeks. When I started this journal, the baseball season seemed so far away and suddenly it is here. I have to admit I'm feeling anxious about what lies ahead. I never dreamed that I could find myself in the position I am now in. I was looking toward law school, and before I knew it, I'm looking at the Yankees, Cubs, Indians and possibly my good old Reds.

There is no question that I have been focused on Brooksie, more than anything else. Just like baseball, I hadn't seen a serious love story as part of my senior year. Yet here we are.

Frankly, I am pretty damned confused. And I'm a little pissed off about it how it is affecting me. But I do know I need to zero in on baseball now.

I am fortunate to have a pal like LT bunking four feet above me in room 204 at Swing Hall. There's no bullshit with LT. But he is also pretty far removed from the potential of signing a contract for some insane money, and also with looking to a future with someone like Nan, who comes from even bigger money.

Last night he gave me some really sage advice. Like always, he looked me dead in the eye and said, "B-3, you're one lucky SOB. All you have to do is look 35 miles down the road to Roselawn and your goddamned parentage. Sit down with Danny Boy, and especially Kayleigh, and let them do their job. You know damned well that you have been blessed with two of the best parents to be found on this fucking planet."

Then he continued by saying, "And by the way, while you clearly don't deserve her, you have somehow landed the smartest and best-looking girl I have ever met. So, don't fuck that up. It seems to me that baseball is the easy part. Just go out there and keep throwing the heat and be sure to find a good accountant. But, like I say, talk to your mom and dad."

Of course, he is right. The only thing he left out was how fortunate I am to have a *cara is fearr* like him (best friend in Gaelic, as my old Gramps used to say).

Right after my talk with LT I called home and spoke with Mom, who answered the phone, and told her I would be coming home for the weekend and would like to schedule a little private time with her and Dad. She took it as if she had been reading my mind and was expecting the need for a little parental therapy.

This works out great on a different front, because Brooksie is meeting her parents in Chicago for the upcoming weekend. The details are too rediculous to list, but they mostly have to do with Bags' business, and shopping and dining for Nan and Queenie. Nuf said!!

Tomorrow is the Flamingo Stakes. So, Bags, Queenie and their nag are in Miami for the big race. A horse named Northern Dancer is the favorite. God help us if Lucky Larry wins.

I'm headed over to Withrow Court to run the steps. One thing I know for sure is that sweating always helps clear my head. Maybe some of our basketball team's success will rub off on me. They have won eight of their last nine games. Go Skins!!

March 9, 1964

((

W ell, my trip home this past weekend was just what the doctor ordered. Liz came home with me. We had a nice family dinner at Howard Johnson's near our home, on Friday night. It was five orders of fried clams for the Boyd clan. The only variable was what flavor of ice cream we ordered for dessert. For me it's always pistachio. My two sisters and Dad hit a double dip chocolate and Mom landed a strawberry. Why any of this is important I could not say.

As to my therapy session, Mom infromed me that this was a family issue and Liz andf Mir should be part of it. Actually I was fine with that. It's the way the Boyds operate. So, it was decided that the Billy Boyd psychoanalysis would take place Saturday moring over French toast with a side of bacon.

After I tried to lay out my current apprehension and discomfort over my situation and what lie ahead, Dad took the first swing by addressing the baseball piece of the equation.

He said to me, "Billy, first don't start thinking you are Sandy Kofax... You are not. You're Billy Boyd with the potential to be just OK, or maybe, some day better than Kofax. Take the journey, do the hard work and find out. The four of us don't love you because of your fastball. There's an old Irish proverb, 'inhale peace, exhale worry.' Take it one day at a time and you'll be fine."

That was all I needed to hear on baseball.

Then Mom handled the more complicated Nancy Brooks conundrum. She began by suggesting that a big part of what was in play was what she called Nouveau Riche syndrome.

To explain she said, "Billy, Lawrence and Francis Brooks are displaying classic behavior of people who had nothing growing up, and then very quickly found incredible wealth. First, you must respect Larry's success. It is impressive. But you must also understand that they are fighting an unachievable battle for social acceptance from people with generations of wealth and social standing."

She continued, "The Porches, the airplanes, the yachts, the way they dress, the way they talk, are all attempts to become something that they are not. Your issue is to determine what the effect of all of this has had on Nancy. Your dad and I have been somewhat dumbfounded by how grounded... how well adjusted... how unaffected she seems to be. For what it is worth, your father and I have been very impressed with her. The Brooks are ostentatious, but it seems that Nancy is not. But we do wonder if there is something we are missing."

Liz jumped in by saying, "Billy, you know I wasn't thrilled with what you did to Toni. But as I've gotten to know Nancy, I really understand. She is special. If you can get her away Lexington and she leaves her wallet at home, it could work out great."

Mom asked, "Have you spoken to her about all of this?"

The answer was easy. Nan and I have discussed this ad nauseam. I shared Nan's admiration for our family and her frustration with her own.

At that point, Dad piped in again. His advice was to take my foot off the gas a little, with trying to make a future with Nan. He suggested that for the rest of the school year my priorities should be my classes and baseball. Those are the current events. Nan is more of a long term adventure. If she is all I think she is, Dad suggested that she would willingly understand. As he said, she was in my life last season... why not try to just repeat that?

Well, I have to admit that by the time the French toast was gone, so was much of my anxiety. I guess sometimes you just need to hear what you already know from those you love the most.

By the way, Lucky Larry finished dead last in the Flamingo Stakes earlier this week and I suspect Bags is in search of a glue factory. Nan reports there will be no trip to the Derby next month. She called me from Chicago Saturday to advise that her father was drowning his sorrows at the Palmer House Bar. Its March, and he is in the Windy City, so he can go fly a kite as far as I'm concerned.

Practice starts a week from today. I'm ready.

Marᴄʜ 15, 1964

{{{

H ey Journal... BEWARE!! It's the crazy wonderful Ides of March baby. So if your name is Brutus you better eat two.

Since we were forced in our senior English class at Woodward to read *Julius Caesar* by this cat you may have heard of... Willy (not Billy) Shakespeare, LT and I have made a big deal over da Ides. It just tickles the shit out of us, for some reason.

The over/under on the number of our football teammates who have even heard about this special day is in single figures... a fact LT proved last year by polling the whole team. LT did point out that the number might be a bit higher this year as last year's seniors were dumber than shit idiots, while this year's sophomores might be significantly brighter morons.

To enhance our fun connected to this special day, LT suggested that we post a piece of paper on the door of every jock in Swing Hall that says "BEWARE" and see if anyone gets it. So far, only Len Billett, our catcher on the baseball team has reacted. He lives two doors down the hall. He busted through our door early this morning with the paper in hand and yelled, "Hail Caesar, Motherfuckers!"

The general response from the rest of the Jock Village has been, "What the hell is this?"

LT's response has been, "I come to bury Caesar, not to praise him."

Nobody got that either.

The baseball season offically starts tomorrow with a workout in the Withrow Court Gym. Physically I am 100% ready. They say the most important thing to a pitcher is leg strength. Hundreds of trips up and down the stadium steps has allowed me to check that box. Plus I know my arm is ready. The only question mark is my head. But that has never been a problem either, once I step on the mound.

When Brooksie returned from Chicago last week we had a serious sitdown. After a weekend of decadence in Chicago with her dipshit parents, she listened to me intently and said sweetly, "Billy, whatever you need me to be, that's what I'll be. I fully understand the importance of the baseball season. I simply love you and just want to be a supportive part of your team."

Tomorrow it starts. Our first game is against Xavier on April 8th. Musketeers, BEWARE!

Now, as much as I get a major giggle out of the Ides, my parents truly believe that St. Patricks Day should be a National Holiday here in the U.S. Frankly, I could care less about some half-assed Saint named Patrick. I don't own a single piece of green clothing. And I hate Bowling Green. I've already made clear my feelings about Notre Dame.

Mom and Dad on the other hand start planning for the big day around the first of each year. The main event is dinner at O'Malley's in the Alley, that is neatly hidden in the alley on West Ogden Place, between 3rd and 4th Streets just west of Vine Street. The tradition started in 1950. The offical plan is Guinness, Jamison's, corned beef, cabbage, Irish apple cake, and singing at the top of their lungs, followed by two days in bed at the Netherland Plaza Hotel. There is no way to be delicate about this. Mom and Dad embrace their Irish roots three days a year. Mom calls in sick at Walnut Hills if any of those magical days fall on a week day. Dad owns the drug store. So, his friend, employee and fellow Pharmacist, Sid Graulich knows he will be rolling solo on March 17-19 every year.

And they make no bones about it. This is serious shit to them. Liz, Mir and I are to leave them alone at all costs. When we were younger, Grams, Ruthie pulled the baby-sitting duties. While Grams doesn't much care for Guinness, she seems to fully understant the hotel room part of the equation. At this point the whole stupid mess has just become quaint.

Dad starts training around St. Valentine's wearing out the Victrola with his Bing Crosby album, *Shillegaghs and Shamrocks*. I'll say this, they always return home from their little sojourn happy. Salainte Mom and Dad. But no green beer for this white boy.

March 18, 1964

W ell, we are two days into practice, and I would say we are off to a great start. On Monday, coach pulled me aside and told me to just relax and let my talent speak for itself. He also reported that he had spoken to his long-time friend, Illinois Wesleyan teammate and Sigma Chi fraternity brother, Bobby Winkles, who is the highly successful baseball coach at Arizona State. Andy admitted he was seeking advice on how best to handle me this upcoming season. He went on to tell me that Winkles said we should start slowly to protect my arm in the cold climate of Oxford Ohio.

Andy said, "Billy, this week I just want you tossing the ball the first few days. Then you can start working on the mound with Billet, but throwing nothing but straight stuff. That should do for a week. Then, we can start with the breaking stuff about ten days in. How does that sound?"

Anyone in college baseball who doesn't know about Bobby Winkles should be ashamed of himself. I was getting some of the best advice available in the college game. So, even though I had been secretly working on my Joe Nuxhall slider, I respectfully looked at Andy and said, "Sure Coach. Sounds good."

So, for the last two days I have been tossing the old rawhide with several of my teammates and taking my turn in the batting cage. Bottom line; I'm relaxed and feeling good.

On a different front, LT told me at dinner Monday that Schembechler had offered him a Graduate Assistant coaching opportunity for next year. The way that works is that LT can start graduate school for free in turn for helping to coach the offensive backfield, while earning a modest stipend. I'll buy a ticket to watch LT try to tell Scotty how to play halfback.

LT said to me, "You know B-3, I think I might like to pursue coaching for real. This smells like a pretty good deal. Plus, it will give me another year to be here around Jan-Mar to see why she has me so confused about women. What do you think, buddy?"

I told my old friend that I thought it was a great thing on all fronts. It's not like he had any solid plan for moving on with his life. He loves football and it might well provide a career path. And he is closer to loving Jan-Mar by a factor of ten than he has been with any other gal he has ever dated. Not to mention, he can find out if he can live within the confines of the ultimatum she gave him a few weeks ago.

Then there's Nan. She hit the first homerun of the season on Saturday. We like to go back quite often to Tuffy's, where our journey began. As we sat there just like on that first day, respectively sipping on a cherry coke and nectar phosphate, she reached across our shiny table, took my hand and said, "Ok Billy, the hour of truth has arrived. We all owe it to you to allow you to take this little journey on the diamond unhindered by any distractions."

She took a sip of coke and continued, "You have become more important to me than anything. My job between now and the end of your season is to support you completely. So, I think we should stay out of hotel rooms and stay far away from Lexington, while concentrating on classes, strike outs and wins. Let's study, hold hands, take long walks, take in some movies and mute discussions about our future. If I do this right, the future will take care of itself. Just please remember every day that I love you and am so proud of you."

Well, fuck me to tears sports fans. If I haven't found the perfect girl... the perfect friend, then I never will.

Bottom line is that everything has fallen into place just when I needed it to line up as straight as the Redskin Marching Band on Homecoming weekend.

I'm feeling lucky and I'm feeling good. Maybe there is a God. (Please don't tell either of my sisters that I wrote that).

March 21, 1964

We had our first intersquad game this morning. Andy let me pitch the first two innings. I gave up a ground ball to shortstop, a lazy fly to centerfield along with four strikeouts. I'm very pleased with how my new slider is coming along. LT, Liz and I drove home to Cincinnati right after I showered, hoping his jalopy would make the 35-mile trip. It did. Brooksie stayed on campus for the weekend noting the need to study for mid-terms.

About an hour after I got home, I received a call from the *Cincinnati Post* sports writer Earl Lawson. He's in Florida covering the Reds, but said that he thinks I am a developing story he'd like to cover. Plus, he admitted that Nuxhall put him on to me.

Lawson is a great reporter who is famous for getting into a fist fight with Reds second baseman Johnny Temple back in 1957, when he was the Red's official scorer. He had charged Temple with an error to which the feisty second baseman took exception. Then two years ago, centerfielder Vada Pinson caught Lawson with a haymaker for something negative he had written. At the time Lawson joked that Pinson had a much better punch than Temple.

Now here I am talking to him, knowing he doesn't pull any punches. I advised Lawson that if we were to talk, I preferred that one of my parents be present.

He quipped that I had better learn to stand on my own if I ever hoped to pitch in the big leagues. I was proud that I had the forethought and courage to say to him, "Mr. Lawson, there's an old Irish proverb that goes, 'If you want to go fast, go alone. If you want to go far, go together.'"

He politely laughed then ask me how I was getting along with Lawrence and Francis Brooks. Now, I sure didn't see that high inside fastball coming. I responded to that doozy by telling him that he was asking about my private life, and that it was private.

Lawson advised me that I was probably entering a period in my life where nothing would be private. But he retracted the question, graciously wished me luck and said he would be in touch again soon.

After hanging up, I found my mother in the kitchen and reported the details of my Earl Lawson phone call. She walked over and softly touched my cheek and said, "Billy, your personal life can be as private as you choose to make it. But it is time we start planning for the storm that is about to begin. I promise, your father and I will do all we can to be sure that you are prepared. You were right to stand up to Lawson. I'm proud that you did"

march 25, 1964

Two weeks from today we open at home against Xavier. I wish it were tomorrow. And, I suppose with the way I'm behaving, LT and Brooksie probably wish we had opened yesterday. Enough of this practice shit already. Will somebody in a black padded suit please yell, "Play Ball!!"

Last night, I mentioned to Nan that Earl Lawson had called me. She had no clue who I was talking about. When I gave her Lawson's credentials and told her he asked me about her parents, she got so agitated that she immediately called Bags and Queenie.

As it turns out, Bags knows Lawson from the horse racing scene. I guess Mr. Lawson follows the ponies, as well as the Miss America contest. All I can say is that Nan informed me that Bags got really pissed off that Lawson ask about him. Brooksie is now very sorry she called her parents.

I haven't heard another peep from Lawson. But I must say the

"Post" reporter was professional. At the same time, I could see why Pinson and Temple both took a swing at him. Just more shit that I don't need.

On a different subject, the main event at Swing Hall today took place in Len Billet's room. Len is shacked up this year with our senior shortstop, Kenny Butkus. Each month they have a big ceremony that is "invitation-only", at which they hang the current centerfold from "Playboy Magazine". Tonight, the spectacular Nancy Scott, *Miss March*, took her place next to Miss February, Nancy Jo Hooper.

Butkus made the serious misjudgment of suggesting that in keeping with the *Nancy* theme, that Miss April might turn out to be a Miami coed named Nancy Brooks. He knew the minute he had uttered it that there was a distinct chance he might be needing an appointment with a dentist.

Not because of me. As the saying goes, *I'm a lover not a fighter*. Not so much when it comes to LT. But we need Kenny, or "The Vacuum Cleaner" as I like to call him, because of his sure hands at short. So, I hurried in between Kenny and LT and said, "Not funny VC (short for Vacuum Cleaner)."

Then to LT, "Now, LT, if I can forgive that empty-headed remark, so can you. Old Butkus will promise to think before he speaks in the future. But, if he ever says anything about Jan-Mar, all of his teeth are fair game."

LT smiled, threw a fake punch at The Vacuum Cleaner and stepped down while Nancy Scott, in all of her glory, went up. Tradition, Swing Hall style, was sustained. So were VC's teeth.

March 28, 1964

Yesterday was the last day of classes as Spring Break has started. While this is a big deal to most Miami students, for me, it has always meant more baseball. While so many of my friends have headed to Ft. Lauderdale, or Miami Beach or just home for a week of frolicking, old Billy Boyd has always been stuck here on campus forced to study the Great American Past Time.

Hey no complaints. I love the American Past Time. Besides, Danny and Kayleigh Boyd aren't going to pony up their hard-earned savings on Florida vacations for their kids. Ask Liz. But my sisters and I know this, and get it.

The good news this year is that LT, Nan and Jan-Mar are staying on campus. We will all try to behave as adults. This will be made more palatable by the fact that LT's hidden bag of bolts is readily available for little side trips. We plan to head to Richmond Indiana tonight for the famous all-you-can-eat buffet at Anderson's. Richmond is an easy forty-minute drive from Oxford up US 27 through the little town of College Corner that sits on the state line. So, there are two College Corners... one in Ohio and one in Indiana. LT calls College Corner a "Head and Plum Town." No sooner do you stick your head in and your plum out!

Anderson's is a losing proposition when LT shows up. That big boy can put away prodigious amounts of food. And he doesn't waste time on lettuce and vegetables. My roomie heads right for the carved roast beef and fried chicken. How they can allow LT to eat a truckload of meat and potatoes followed by a boatload of desserts for a buck, makes no sense. They will make up some of their loses on Brooksie and Jan-Mar, and maybe break even on me.

But heads-up Anderson's, LT is headed your way.

I am very happy that my roomie along with my gal Nan and her roomie Jan-Mar will all be around this coming week. Having to hang out with nothing but baseballers is just too much baseball. Per usual, Queenie is pissed. She wanted to take Nan shopping in New York while Bags stayed in Lexington to count his money. I know this is bad, but I love when Brooksie pisses off her mother.

Tomorrow is Easter. I hope all my friends can find their eggs whether it be in Ft. Lauderdale or here on campus. A big day for Huge Hefner. If you're looking for real attractive Bunnies, there's eight of them hanging on the wall in the Butkus/Billet room, two doors down.

To all of the vacationing Redskins... drive safely!!

APRIL 1, 1964

W ell, sports fans, it's April first... No fooling. Another special day at Swing Hall for sure for those of us who have stayed on campus. A lot of April fooling around by a lot of Joe College fools. The pranks have abounded all day. For example, when I got back to my room after practice this afternoon, I discovered that my favorite picture of Brooksie that sat framed on my desk, had been replaced by one of Groucho Marx, eyebrows raised with a corona neatly stuffed in his mustached decorated chops. Very funny LT. I must say that our preseason practices are going very well. I gained All-American honors last year with just a fastball, a curve and my floater. But I am very pleased with my new wrist supination infested slider. I truly feel that I have a new and important weapon. LT has joked that if I get a big signing bonus, Nuxhall should deserve a cut. And he isn't wrong about that.

Speaking of cuts, I need to cut this short, as Nan, LT, Jan-Mar and

I are headed uptown to see the new Peter Sellers flick, Dr. Strangelove. LT and I have become huge Peter Sellers fans since seeing him last year in The Pink Panther. That film was truly hilarious. Strange Love is supposed to be a spoof of nuclear war. Can't wait to see how they pull that off.

At any rate, it's Brooksie, Peter Sellers and buttered corn coming up to bat. LT has promised not to get any butter on Jan-Mar's blouse... if you get my drift?

APRIL 2, 1964

W ell, the movie last night wasn't what I had expected. Jan-Mar called it "dark comedy" and she wasn't whistling Dixie.

The movie proved to be a thought-provoking satire about what is often referred to as the *Cold War*. It was both hilarious and frightening. It had an interesting cast. Peter Sellers plays multiple roles, including the wheel-chair bound Dr, Strangelove who is clearly a secret Nazi who suffers from "alien hand", an instinct to raise his arm in a *sieg heil* salute.

A crazed, and sexually impotent, American General, played by Sterling Hayden, plans to launch a nuclear attack on the Soviet Union. Eventually, that hayseed actor, Slim Pickens, playing Air Force Major, T.J. "King" Kong hops upon a nuclear bomb as if it were a bucking bronco and gloriously rides it to his death. The movie ends with Strangelove suddenly rising from his wheelchair exclaiming, "Mein Fuhrer, I can walk," as the WWII song, "We'll Meet Again," by Vera

Lynn, plays in the background.

When the lights came up, LT looked at Jan-Mar, still wearing a spotless blouse, and said, "What the hell was that?"

She patted him on the head and said, "We will explain it to you when you grow up, big guy."

Bottom line is, it was a funny, yet thought provoking movie. We ended last night by strolling across the street to Al and Larry's discussing the film and the potential for atomic war, over ice teas and cokes. Jan-Mar nixed LT's attempt to order onion rings, telling him he could have them when he was flying solo on an atom bomb.

One thing we all agreed upon is that the damned movie had us thinking about the 1962 Cuban Missile Crisis again. Baseball didn't seem so important for a few moments.

Brooksie, being the only intellect in our little posse, pointed out that there was only one female character in the movie, and of course, she played somebody's mistress. This was followed by a small rant about how it is a man's world and men insist on objectifying women.

I held my tongue, and did not remind her that there is nothing much more objectifying than beauty contests, knowing that she already agreed that Bags pretty much saw Queenie as a plaything.

LT, unable to hold his tongue, told Jan-Mar that she was the object of his affection. To her credit, Brooksie laughed along with the rest of us.

Then LT provided more giggles when he stated that his favorite part of the evening was the Road Runner cartoon. "Meep meep!!"

The final April Fool's joke of the day came when LT dropped to a knee at Al and Larry's and asked Jan-Mar to marry him.

Always quick on the draw, Jan-Mar shot right back at him, "April Fucking Fools Lenny Boy. Get back to me when you have a job and a diamond."

APrIL 5, 1964

C lasses resume tomorrow. Today is Sunday, so no practice. Once again, as it has been for about a year of Sundays, you won't be finding Brooksie and me in church... Sorry Jesus. Bags and Queenie have always skirted *church-going* by sending a big check each year to the Main Street Baptist Church in downtown Lexington. Nan is certain that her father truly believes he can buy his way into heaven without any pew time.

Now, my religious background is fairly diverse with a passel of Irish Catholics and a few Ashkenazi Jews sprinkled in. I have often heard Grams Ruthie joke about coming from a Jewish sect who's last four letters are *NAZI*. If you knew Grams you would understand why so many comedians are Jewish.

There is a big part of my Irish family who have scored a bunch of *Hail Marys* and have strong right arms from all of their genuflecting. But as to our little immediate clan, the Irishness has been limited to

Guinness, Harps, Jameson's, Bing Crosby on St. Paddy's Day and four-leaf-clovers. Dad does often say that Jamison's is a good *Catholic Whiskey... only Baptist drink Bushmills*. So, *Slainte* Bags! Go easy on the Bushmills, asshole. Whoops, got a little carried away there. Anyway, that explains why Brooksie and I have the *no-church* element in common.

We haven't seen LT and Jan-Mar since Friday afternoon, but they haven't been in church. They headed to our favorite Hamilton hotel, and probably haven't seen the light of day all weekend. But in keeping with Nan's promise, we have been staying out of hotel rooms since practice started. Not that it hasn't entered my mind. After practice yesterday, Andy announced his starting lineup for our opener against Xavier on Wednesday. On paper we look very solid. Here's the batting order the old coacher posted:

Senior	Mike Lindsay	2nd Base
Junior	Wally Pittman	Left Field
Sophomore	Freddie Cohen	Third Base
Senior	Len Billet	Catcher
Junior	Henry Kwiatkwoski	1st Base
Senior	Billy Boyd	Pitcher
Senior	Kenny Butkus	Short Stop
Senior	Jerry Morris	Center Field
Junior	Eddie Fulton	Right Field

So, that's it. I will start the first game. This will make me available to pitch again on Saturday in our second of two games against Marshall. We are fortunate to be starting the season with three home games. Then we head to Ohio State.

I appreciate Andy letting me hit sixth in this lineup. I can say modestly, that I remain one of the best hitters on the team.

We will be going with a three-man rotation. Our junior lefty, Marco Bellini and sophomore righthander, Bobby Conn will be on the mound when I'm not. Coach Anderson, who doesn't readily hand out compliments, has called the three of us the best starting rotation he has ever had at Miami. We have some guys that can really handle the lumber stepping up to the plate as well. And all of this is rounded out by lefty, Chad Schmidt and righthander, Spike Chandler in the bull pen.

We really feel we can give Ohio University and Western Michigan a good run for the Mid-American Conference championship this year. It's pretty damned exciting.

The only thing left to report is that Brooksie and I hitched a ride down to Cincinnati this morning with Maggie Greenlee, a friend of Nan's at Wells Hall. We spend the day at, what my late grandfather Liam Boyd used to call, *Abhaile Boy*d (the Boyd Home).

We arrived just in time for my mother's Sunday brunch. Today it was scrambled eggs, waffles and rashers. Now rashers are interesting. They are an Irish version of bacon made from the more palatable loin of the hog. Thus, it is leaner than traditional bacon. But it is a tradition that has become hard to come by. About once a month, my mother runs down to Findlay Market, where, once inside, she heads to O'Reilly's Meat Stand. It is the only place left in Cincinnati where she can still get rashers, bangers and mutton. She insists on mutton for her Guinness Stew. And she often just braises mutton served with potatoes and carrots.

But enough about being Irish. Mom just loves to cook and has passed the passion on to Mir and Liz. Nan is slowly learning to eat all of this strange shit, and always pitches in to help.

Over the food today, the conversation turned to my grandparents,

Liam and Bahny Boyd and Patrick and Ruth Broderick. It is really sad that Brooksie never had the chance to know my two grandfathers. They were both solid, second-generation Americans, grateful to have had the benefits of citizenship. And they were both what the Irish would call *greannmahr sean-fhear* (funny old man). I prefer to use the Jewish version. They were hilarious *alte kakers*.

The main point is that the Boyds and the Brodericks had seemingly perfect marriages. For that reason, I wanted Nan to know more about them. The stories flowed happily and freely. Mom reminisced about their Saturday night card games. For about a dozen years after the war the four of them would get together most Saturday nights for pinochle and later canasta. Talk about some good Catholic whiskey (Jameson's). Liam and Paddy could throw back that shit.

Sadly, there is not enough Irish whiskey on the planet to create a weekly Canasta game between Mom, Dad, Bags and Queenie, even if they lived next door to each other (which they never will). Oh well. Actually, it was Brooksie that made that point earlier tonight when we got back to Oxford. But she had a great time visiting with the Boyds of Cincinnati.

APrIL 8, 1964

The big day has arrived, and I have my first win and shut out, of the 1964 season. I gave up three inconsequential hits, two on curve balls and a double on a slider that didn't slide much. But other than the one errant pitch, my control was spot on. And my heat was hot. I also had two hits and one RBI at the plate. Final score; Miami 9 – Xavier 0.

I guess the real story for me was the crowd that showed up. When I first suited up at Miami, you could find more cigars in a box of Ibolds than fans in the stands. I am told that Miami Field can comfortably seat approximately 850 fans. I am also told that it had never been filled to capacity until I had tossed a couple of *no-nos* (no hitters) last year.

After the game today, Miami Information Director, Bob Kurz, came up to my locker to advise me they had sold more than 1,800 tickets, over half of them 50 cent standing-room-only babies, plus 862 one-dollar grandstand seats. He also explained that there was 14 people from the press at the little table behind the plate, along with 11 scouts from various major league teams, that Miami lets in gratis.

Kurz said to me, standing at my locker, "Billy, thanks to you, the baseball program may pay for itself for the first time ever. I'm told that we scored $1,388 today. That's a record by a bunch."

I let that sink in and quickly decided that I didn't need to be sharing that information with anybody other than my little journal here. You see, I have a certain built-in modesty, manufactured early in my childhood by Daniel and Kayleigh Boyd and reinforced by all four of my grandparents. Our whole lives, Liz, Mir and I have been told that self-confidence is important while narcissism is abhorrent.

Now, at this point in my life, never has that message been more important. I thought back to the conversation that I had with Mom a couple of weeks ago after I had spoken with Earl Lawson. She and Dad had kept the promise she had made that day.

When Brooksie and I were at home this past Sunday we had what Dad likes to call a *Clan Bake*. That is when they gather my sisters and me together for a heart-to-heart. On Sunday, Mom insisted that Nan be a part of this process. The basic theme was that I was going to get far more attention than I deserved in a sane world. But like all heroes, sports stars are elevated way too high for their own good.

It is my job to see that I not let that happen. It is the job of the rest of my family to make absolutely sure that I don't get too full of myself as a result of wins, strikeouts, sellout crowds and an over-zealous press. I knew that it was especially important to Mom that Nan understand and sign off on this. She did. Now, after our first game with scouts and sports writers starting to clamor around me, it was time to put that plan into action. And, by the way, I have a pal I call LT, who sure as hell is going to keep me in line.

Next up, Marshall.

APrIL 12, 1964

W ell, our sophomore starter Bobby Conn got his first start Friday and was so good he had our fans forgetting about me. He shut out Marshall, giving up only four hits. More importantly, he struck out sixteen of the so-called *Thundering Herd*. Bobby is a great kid and I was very happy to see him win in his debut. So was Andy, the old coacher. Nothing a coach loves better than a great sophomore.

Then I came back yesterday and threw a one hitter, depriving the *Herd* of their *Thunder*. They have a little second baseman they call Rocky Richards. That little bastard, choking three inches up on his Louisville Slugger, slapped one of my best fast balls, that was two inches outside, up the middle, for Marshall's only hit. I should be pissed, but with my no-hitter ruined, some of the big crowd at the game was able to rush the fifty yards over to the track when they announced the mile run. And for good reason.

You see Miami has a track star who is, in my opinion, much more impressive, than yours truly, Billy Broderick Boyd. Bob Shul is a threat to run a four-minute mile every time he steps into the starting blocks, and if he does, there's a passel of fans who want to see it. Hell, I want to see it.

More importantly, Bob is quite likely to be running the 5,000-meter race at this year's Olympic games in Tokyo. He is ranked second in the world behind some French cat.

In this morning's *Cincinnati Enquirer,* sports writer, Jim Schottelkotte reported, in the same story that, "World Class Runner, Bob Shul ran a 4 minute, 2.6 second mile while the Magnificent Fast-Baller, Billy Boyd" tossed a one hitter." He suggested that there was a distinct possibility that before season's end, on the same day, Miami fans could be treated to a sub-four-minute-mile and a no-hitter, occurring less than a hundred yards apart. The article concluded with, "It was a special day in Oxford."

It's funny. When I read my name in the newspapers, I'm a little bothered with "Billy." I'm not sure that this is what I wish to be called as an adult. I mean, I'm used to hearing it. It's been my name all of my life. I certainly don't care for "William" or just plain "Bill". And you can't go through life answering to "Gunner" or "B-3." But when Schottelkotte writes, "fast-baller Billy Boyd" it sounds pretty juvenile.

I mentioned this to both LT and to Brooksie earlier today. LT just said, "Fuck that, B-3. You got bigger fish to fry. Billy Boyd is a great sports name. You don't see Billy Martin bitching about it. Your fucking name is in the fucking *Enquirer*. Next year it might be in the *Chicago Tribune*, or the *New York Times,* or the fucking *Boston Globe*. You gotta be shitting me. You're fucking Billy Boyd. Nuf said!"

Brooksie was a little more gentle. She smiled that wonderful ray of sunshine smile of hers and said, "I love Billy Boyd. But if I have too, I can love "William" or "Bill" just as much. But I agree with LT, Billy

Boyd sounds like a Major League pitcher to me."

Well, fuck me to tears, I guess I am "Billy Fucking Boyd" and should probably quit reading the papers.

So, no complaints about how we have started the season. We are three and 0, with two wins in league play. We head to Ohio State Tuesday to take on the Buckeyes. I really wanted to start that game, as the Big Ten isn't called "Big" for nothing. Bob Kurz told me that Ohio State is ranked second in the Big Ten behind a really good Minnesota Gophers team. My only hope to see any action in Columbus is if Andy asks me to pinch hit. Sometimes I miss centerfield.

But I will start next Friday against Bowling Green, in a more important league game. And Andy has promised to give me the ball again on the 21st when we mosey on down to Cincinnati to play the Bearcats. So, no complaints.

You may not believe this, but Brooksie and I missed church again today. LT, like Nan and me, is a card-carrying heathen. The three of us have managed to totally corrupt Jan-Mar, who was a good Christian church-goer when she first showed up on campus. Thanks to our little trio of Philistines, Jan-Mar hasn't set foot in the Oxford United Methodist Church the entire school year. But, as LT likes to point out, she has spent more than a few Sunday mornings this year in the *Church of You Show Me Yours and I'll Show You Mine*.

Jan-Mar is interesting in that she is a legitimate southerner. We have listened to her talk often, in her Scarlet O'Hara accent (which LT loves by the way), about her upbringing and how important the Methodist Church was to her parents. I have also heard her say that her father is a true lifetime subscriber to *manifest destiny*, and that it would be a huge mistake to mess with the big guy upstairs. Like so many southerners, her parents truly believe that the good old USA belongs to white Christians. To her credit, she has often stated that she has always been uncomfortable with that premise. Coming to Miami has done much to help her break the bonds of that Deep South bullshit.

These days she jokes that it has been Nan, LT and me who have finished the job of turning her into a modern, broad-minded liberal gal. She now agrees there's a better way of spending Sunday mornings than sitting on a hardwood bench with a book of fiction in her hands, saying amend every 30 seconds. So, look at it this way. We've saved Jan-Mar a passel of Abe Lincolns that would have otherwise wound up in the collection basket. Praise Lord and pass the biscuits!

APRIL 15, 1964

I t seemed to take forever for the baseball season to get here. Now suddenly it is racing by like Parnelli Jones on the Indianapolis Speedway.

And yesterday we crashed and burned at Ohio State. The Buckeyes scalped the Redskins by a lopsided score of 11-1. Len Billet smashed one over the centerfield fence to save us from being shutout.

Of course, Andy was really pissed. He is pretty good friends with Ohio State coach Marty Karow who is a bit of a legend at OSU, second only to Woody Hayes. Karow was a standout football and baseball player for the Buckeyes, and played briefly in the big leagues. Andy really hates losing to friends. It was a quiet bus ride back to Oxford I can tell you.

Any leftover silence was broken this morning, when Pauly Biadasz opened our door and farted the Miami fight song. That's right, Badass has such sphincter control that he can literally fart simple tunes. His list of ass-hits include:

- *Row, Row, Row, Your Boat*

- *Mary Had a Little Lamb*

- *Twinkle Twinkle Little Star*

- *Jingle Bells*

- *Love Me Tender*

- *Happy Birthday*

LT loves this and has suggested that Pauly cut an album titled "Gas from the Ass of Pauly Badass." My roomie has also advocated for Pauly to attach a microphone to his talented behind and join the brass section of the Miami Marching Band.

For his part, Pauly often says to his fellow jocks over breakfast, "Beans are for melody, eggs are for fragrance."

At any rate, Pauly's half-ass attempt to break the doldrums of yesterday's loss, worked. Laughter cures a lot of ills, including getting your ass kicked on the ballfield.

Now, it is up to me to turn things around at the U. of Cincinnati on Saturday. I plan to do just that. The only downside is that Bags and Queenie have decided to fly his little Christmas gift to himself up to Lunken airport Saturday morning to see for themselves if old B-3 can pitch.

To her credit, Our Miss Brooks called Mom to invite her and Dad to join them for dinner Saturday night at the Gourmet Room, atop the Terrace Plaza Hotel. For Bags and Queenie this will complete their Cincinnati fine-dining *hat trick*.

Fortunately, for Mom and Dad, they are committed to having

dinner after the game Saturday with New York Yankee scout, Tom Greenwade. This is the guy that signed Mickey Mantle. What do you think about that Bags?

Since Greenwade asked Mom to pick a place, I can assure you that snails and sturgeon eggs will not be on the menu. My parents have opted for the more mundane, Wig Wam Restaurant in the suburbs. But it is one fine eatery. Great food and great ambiance, at half the price.

I have totally handed off the Big-League Scout piece of my life to Mom and Dad. Greenwade is the first scout with whom they have engaged beyond the phone call stage. Dad said the Yankee scout was a perfect gentleman and very professional. His discussion with my parents has not been about money, but rather why the Yankees are the right answer for their right-handed son.

One thing for sure is that the Boyd family has entered into something we never could have imagined back when I was a Woodward Bulldog.

APRIL 19, 1964

Yeah baby!! Big day yesterday. We have a saying at Miami. There are three kinds of games: One is a home game. One is an away game. The third, and most important, are games against the University of Cincinnati Bearcats. Hell, there is Victory Bell, that the winning team, in the oldest football rivalry in the country, rings each year if they win. And the Redskins have done a lot of ringing lately.

After I threw my first fastball past the leadoff batter yesterday, I knew I was in a special groove. Less than two hours later I had pitched a *Perfect Game*, with only one ball leaving the infield all day. Twenty-seven batters up... twenty-seven batters down.

Even Andy joined in the celebration when my 17th strikeout ended the game. All of this in front several scouts, a bunch of sports writers, a couple of dozen of my Cincinnati friends, Mom, Dad, Liz, Mir, LT, Bags, Queenie, Nan and Jan-Mar. And, low and behold, also Jan-Mar's Mom and Dad, who are in town and pinch hit for my parents at the Gourmet Room last night.

On page three of the "Sunday Enquirer" this morning was the bold headline, PERFECT! Jim Schottelkotte, who was at the game, wrote the glowing piece, which included a quote from the UC coach, Glenn Sample, who said, "That kid is special. You never want to lose. But he pitched like a Major League All-Star. You have to respect, and even enjoy seeing, that kind of baseball talent."

Brooksie and Jan-Mar joined the food fest at the Gourmet Room last night. They both fully understood when LT and I opted out of sucking back oysters and shrimp cocktail the size of a gym shoe. There was just too much going on. Instead, we went for breaded veal cutlet with some of our Cincinnati boys at Paradise Gardens on Sixth Street. Of course, Bags and Queenie could have cared less.

I will say this, Jan-Mar's parents are delightful. They are loaded with both southern charm and leftover confederate money. They dress tastefully and have a level of personal polish that the Brooks will never achieve. But then, neither will I. You can't buy that shit at a horse auction or at Boyd's Pharmacy. But, again, that contrast between the Marleys and the Brooks raises the question, how did Nan ever develop her own sweetness and softness? It may be an unanswerable question.

When LT dropped me at home last night, I sat down with Mom and Dad in our kitchen to discuss their dinner with Tom Greenwade. Dad explained that the scout had two strong arguments for considering the Yankees. First Greenwade had discussed the strength of their Farm System. Second, he described why it could be a fast track to the Bigs with the Yankees for a right- handed fastballer like me. While the Yankees have a great pitching staff, they are not a bunch of spring chickens hurling the rawhide. So, opportunity should abound over the next five years.

And, as Mom pointed out, there was one other point her new pal

Tom made. The Yankees have won twenty World Series since 1920. Greenwade looked my mother dead in the eye and said, "There's a reason they wrote that musical, *Damn Yankees*."

And, the thing that impressed Mom and Dad most, is that once again, Greenwade didn't try to win them over with money. His only reference to dough was when he said that I was going to be offered a ton of greenbacks. He promised that the Yankees would make a fair offer. Then, when Dad asked him for a round number, he responded by saying the Yankees would not be making an offer until the season had finished, and that it was best that I not be distracted with money worries. He finished by saying April and May are about pitching. June will be about money. The Yankees will bring their checkbook to Oxford the day the season ends for the Redskins.

I could tell that, with Mom and Dad, Greenwade had moved the Yankees to the top of the list. Yankee Stadium or Crosley Field? Tommy boy is right... it's a damned distraction. And I'll have all week to dwell on the BS.

We have Dayton at home Tuesday and that will be Marco Bellini's problem. Marco got his ass handed to him at Ohio State. But Dayton is loaded with lefthanded batters. So, they match up with Marco's Italian curve ball.

I go again next on Friday when we head to Bowling Green. LT reminded me that it is one of the great "pick-up" campuses in the Mid-America Conference. Now there's a distraction I don't need. He promised not to share that league intelligence with Brooksie.

For now, I plan to float in the glory of my first perfect game, while trying to contain my ego and not think about wearing Yankee pinstripes someday.

LT has suggested that I go to sleep and dream about "Brooksie's perfect mammaries."

Often when a well-endowed coed passes by, he will break into the famous Bob Hope Theme Song, "Thanks for the Memories." Except he sings, "Thanks for the Mammaries." My roomie is a pig. A funny pig... but a pig with a capital Oink!

APrIL 26, 1964

((

It has been a good week, baseball speaking. We easily beat Dayton on Tuesday. Then we took two from Bowling Green Friday and yesterday. I had good stuff on Friday. But I did give up my first run of the year on a homerun by BG's centerfielder, whose name has a record number of syllables and a bunch of "Ks". All, I know is that I hung a curve ball and he hung that sumbitch off of a clothesline hanging from a women's dorm that overlooks left field, about a mile away.

It was a good thing in a way. After watching him do his homerun trot, I was able to bare down and only allowed one more hit. Bobby Conn handled BG in game two yesterday.

We got back to Oxford last night around 9:30, and I hustled my Irish behind up to Al and Larry's where LT, Jan-Mar and Brooksie were into their third 3.2 beer. Oxford is a semi-dry town. No hard liquor and only 3.2 beer. It is sort of a training camp for future alcoholics.

I was particularly excited to see Nan. Things have been just a little off since baseball started and she made her pronouncement not to get in the way of my journey. Before that, everything was evolving so naturally, where it seemed we had both found a great rhythm. We are still very connected. But I feel like I am experiencing a serious case of romance hiccups.

While our little group was slamming back three Budweiser's and an ice tea (me), Nan announced that Bags had called her Saturday morning to see how my game had gone on Friday. She advised me that after Bags and Queenie had witnessed my *No-No Perfection* at UC, they had suddenly become huge Billy Boyd fans.

When she saw my response to that, she laughed her cute little giggle and said, "Billy, if you need an agent, Daddy's law firm is standing by."

My immediate response was, "The only agents I need are in Roselawn."

She kissed me firm on the lips, and told me not to be so damned serious. For what it is worth, she is happy that her parents were starting to see some value in me. I thought, without saying it, their new-found respect probably had a lot more to do with my market value than my strength of character.

But then, I look at Nan and I see my future. Even more so than I can see baseball in my future. Marriage someday, has always made sense. All I have had to do is look at my parents and grandparents, and there is the road map. Fame as an athlete, as much as I love baseball and football, never registered as something as a real expectation.

LT has always said, if you are starting to have serious feelings for a girl, you better check out their mother because that's what you will be married to in thirty years. On the "looks" front, Queenie is hard to beat. But she seems so shallow compared to my mother. Yet I see none of that shallowness in Brooksie.

Enough of this self-analysis BS. I closed out the night with a 3.2 Red Label. Thanks Mabel. Just one more point. LT reports that Jan-Mar's mom has passed the *Middle-age Look Test*. That Georgia Peach is sneaking up on him.

APrIL 30, 1964

We had back-to-back non-league road games on Tuesday and Wednesday. Marco took to the mound at Butler University Tuesday in Indianapolis. He was in good form as we beat the Bulldogs easily by a score of 11-2. The highlight of the day was seeing the Butler Fieldhouse. For a small school, their gym is a cathedral. And there's a lot of history there. Let's just say it beats the shit out of Withrow Court where I maintain a locker for football and baseball. On the other hand, the Butler campus looks like a slum compared to Miami.

After the game at Butler, we bused our way down to the little town of Bloomington, the home of Indiana University. We stayed at the Hotel Rogers on the south edge of downtown Bloomington. When we do an overnight, I bunk with our catcher and team character, Len Billet. Without Len, I'd be looking for different work in June. He was key to my pitching success. His patience and encouragement got me through the early days two years ago.

He keeps the team loose with his silliness and constant joking. His first attempt, at dinner tonight, with our whole starting lineup at the same big round table, was this beaut:

> *So, the local postman was retiring. The neighbors on Spring Street all agreed to give him a little something on his last day. He gets to the last house and is met by the beautiful Mrs. Smith dressed in a see-through negligee. She invites him upstairs for an hour of serious sex. When they finished, she gave him a dollar bill. As the mailman was leaving, Mr. Smith walked in. He looked at his nude wife and asked what the hell was going on. She explained that it was his idea. "What do mean my idea" he demanded. She snaped right back at him, "When I told you all the neighbors were going to do something for him, you said 'fuck him, give him a dollar!'"*

After the laughter, Len looked at me and said, "Here's one for you Gunner. Your dad's a pharmacist, right?"

Without waiting for me to answer, he said, "*Did you hear about the sign in the window of Boyd Drugs? It says, For the girl who has everything, we carry penicillin.*"

Len keeps things loose. And that is good for most pitchers.

Andy suggested that with a bunch of Big Ten fastball hitters at Indiana, he would like to see me go with my new slider more often and throw the knuckleball after a fastball a few times. It was almost as if Coach knew what he was doing. I pitched a three hit shutout and we beat the Hoosiers 3-0.

Mom and Dad drove up to Bloomington for the game. We had a brief visit after my shower before I had to hop on the Greyhound bus marked CHARTER. They reported that they had spoken on Monday with scouts from Kansas City, Detroit and the White Sox. Dad assured me they had everything under control and I should continue to concentrate on my pitching. The bus ride back, including a quick stop for dinner outside Columbus Indiana, took over four hours. So, Brooksie was in Wells Hall *curfew jail* by the time we arrived at Withrow Court.

LT and I talked into the wee hours of the morning about our girlfriends and our future. On both counts, right now, his life seems much less complicated than mine. But he pointed out that some of the complications would likely make me a shitload of money. Before we hit the light, he said to me, "B-3 you need to be finding you a good lawyer and a Swiss bank account."

We head to Toledo tomorrow morning, for our typical two-game series with another Mid-America Conference rival. I will be back on the mound Saturday. April is behind us and tomorrow is May Day. But no frolicking around the May Pole for me. I'll be busing up to Tootlydoo as LT calls it. Then I have a big test in my Government 302 class on Monday and I'm ready for both the Rockets and the test.

The finish line for both my college academic and athletic careers is in view, and it is coming at me like one of my own fastballs.

May 3, 1964

I 'll be an SOB if it didn't snowed in Toledo yesterday. I kid you not. We were up 7-0 starting the seventh inning. The home-plate umpire obviously forgot his long-John's and called the game on account of sleet. It was thirty-eight degrees at game time and below freezing when I registered my 8th strike out to end the sixth inning. At any rate, it was two more wins for the Skins in Toledo.

Friday's game, played in acceptable fifty-degree weather, went the full nine innings with the good guys (us) winning by a score of 5-2. So, we remain undefeated in league play.

Andy didn't want me pitching in that kind of weather. But I prevailed, telling him that the half dozen scouts there, freezing their asses off, weren't looking to sign a pussy.

Thanks to the cold, sleet and heavy wind, we were on the team bus headed south by 3:30. Somewhere just north of Sydney, the weather broke and we were safely back in Oxford by 7:45.

LT, Brooksie and Jan-Mar were shocked to see me walk into Al and Larry's so early. Nan proved that she knew how to reward a good surprise by planting one of her prize-winning smackers on my chapped lips. Ouch! Did I mention that it snowed in Toledo?

I am going to make this short, as our little quartet is headed down to Hamilton for a late breakfast. What I can say is, with or without snow, our Redskins are undefeated in the conference and we are getting noticed. A story about us with the headline "Sleet Can't Cool Boyd Heat" appeared on page one of the *Cincinnati Enquirer Sports Section*, right beneath the lead story regarding the Kentucky Derby, which was won yesterday by a Canadian Chestnut steed named Northern Dancer. Lucky Larry was back in Bag's Lexington barn sucking back oats, while Bags was on the same property sucking back Kentucky bourbon and licking his wounds.

It's pancake time. Hamilton, here comes Billy Boyd.

Later, Sunday May 3, 1964

As I mentioned, this morning the four of us employed LT's magnificent driving machine to scurry down to Hamilton where we ordered a hearty breakfast at Frisch's, home of the Big Boy. I took the opportunity to report that, on my return from Toledo, I had found in my mail an acceptance to the University of Cincinnati Law School. Before my totally unexpected success on the pitcher's mound, it had always been my intention to go to law school. Before the Yankees came knocking, Mom, Dad and I had agreed that I should apply to Michigan, Ohio State and Northwestern. But there has been considerable knocking lately, and obviously our focus has changed.

None-the-less, for giggles, I took the Law School Aptitude test last summer, scored very well and secretly applied to Cincinnati Law School in early March. And voila, I have been accepted. LT joked that this gave me some serious leverage with all incoming scouts. Either they pay me big, or, I show them that I will not be pushed around. I've been accepted to Law School, you SOBs.

While LT continued to tease, suggesting that I might be headed to the Supreme Court instead of the American League, I noted a sudden change in Brooksie. And I immediately knew why. She was major league pissed that I had not shared my law school pursuits with her.

Per usual, when she gets angry her first instinct is to become a turtle or a snail and go into her shell. But I also know that there is a tiger in there that will bust out with a vengeance when she is ready. So, I prepared myself for the roar.

Normally, she would wait until we are alone. Not this time. That turtle turned into a jungle cat like something LT and Jan-Mar had not before seen.

She laid into me something fierce, almost driven to tears. *After all she had done to support me over the past year, how dare I keep this from her.* I had no good answer, and before I could devise something feeble, she was gone.

Jan-Mar grabbed my arm and strongly suggested that I would be better served to give Nan some space, and turn my focus to the pancakes that were turning cold in front of me.

Finally, Jan-Mar advised LT and me that the best option might be for her to go find Nan and plead my case. LT and I exchanged looks of agreement and Jan- Mar headed off to do the dirty work. Five minutes later they walked back into Frisch's, sat back down and silently finished their cold breakfasts.I have decided I still have a lot to learn about women. We drove back to campus without a word from anyone. When we finally got to Wells Hall, Brooksie said, "Billy Boy, we're going to take a walk."

After more than an hour strolling the southern quad of the Miami campus, my Bluegrass Belle had set me straight big time and I wasn't thinking of baseball, law school or any other damned thing, except being true-bluer than Kentucky bluegrass. It hadn't entered my mind, but I really had screwed the pooch with this one. Fuck law school.

However, I'm just beating around the bush here. The jackpot of all of this is, that while Nan was giving me down the road, she said to me, "Billy, you are lucky. I have to cut you a break on this law school stuff, because I have a little secret of my own. I have been considering spending the summer in Paris, and I don't mean Paris Kentucky. I should have told you this sooner."

Per usual, my reaction was wrong. "Paris? What the hell Nan. You want to disappear to Europe for the summer?"

She came right back with, "Billy, what difference does that make? Who knows where you're going to be? One thing is for sure, no matter who you sign with, you will be travelling from one hick town to the next, hoping that next year you might upgrade to bigger hick towns. What do you expect me to do? Get an apartment in Birmingham or Pittsfield and hope you might show up? Or, worse yet, spend the summer with my parents in Lexington? This is something we should have discussed months ago and haven't."

She took my hand and continued, "And don't tell LT, because Jan will be going with me and she hasn't told him yet. Actually, summer in Paris was her idea. Her dad can get us a great apartment in Montmartre. And my dad has agreed to pony up enough Francs for me to be able to travel around Europe a bit via Eurail."

I asked her if this was a done deal and she advised me that she and Jan-Mar were scheduled to leave for France on June 14th, a week after my graduation. Suddenly it seemed like her secret was bigger than mine and that was probably why she reacted to mine the way she had. She had been carrying this for a while and reacted out of guilt.

At two-o'clock, Brooksie kissed me hard and sent me on my way. After apologizing and saying that she loved me, she suggested that I would be able to give my full attention to professional baseball without having her as a distraction all summer. It wasn't until I was back in the dorm that it hit me that Brooksie and I were basically guilty of the same crime. But she had walked free and I was on probation. What the hell?

Now I'm not sure what to do about an even bigger secret I have been carrying for a while... I have been shopping for a diamond with one of Dad's golfing buddies, Max Saurer at Saurer's Jewelry downtown on 8th Street, planning to pull the trigger when my presumed big signing bonus hits my bank account. Yeah, what the hell!! I guess I better concentrate on the baseball diamond. Sauer's diamond and Nan will have to wait.

May 4, 1964

B efore the goddamn French got into my head, I had been concentrating on baseball and classes. And that was because Nan
had been good to her word and worked hard at not being a distraction.
Well, that changed big time yesterday. And all I have been able to think
of all day is Brooksie and the Eiffel Tower.

We play Xavier in Cincinnati tomorrow and fortunately I'll be
sitting in the bullpen thinking of Nan and the Arch de Triomphe.
We will stay overnight and play the Bearcats on Wednesday, where
I again will ride the timber and try to get the term, *ooh-la-la* out of
my head, because I will be pitching against the undefeated Kent State
Golden Flashes on Friday. So, screw Maurice Chevalier and let's dash
the Flash. Nobody saw Kent State and us leading the MAC at this
point in the season. But here we are.

The only good news is that my Government 301 exam this morning
was pathetically easy and I am certain that I aced it. I'm thinking

I might have been better off if I had taken *Behavioral Science* this semester. Too late now. I'll have to continue with the on-the-job training.

With Nan, I'm waiting for the other shoe to drop. After promising not to tell LT about Paris, of course, the first thing I did this morning at breakfast was to break the news to him.

But it will probably be OK. My roomy is one cool SOB. First, he was totally unfazed with the news, suggesting that he and Jan-Mar could probably use a break, rather than screwing each other to death, or, out of love, whichever came first. Second, he assured me that his acting skills would save the day when Jan-Mar got around to breaking the news.

"B-3, did you know that my middle name is Marlon?" he asked me. "As in Brando, baby!! Just go ahead and get me an Oscar for my mantle. No sweat, Gunner. I've got you covered. You just be sure you kick their sorry asses up at Kent State on Friday."

If I'm going to accomplish that feat, I need to get my head around Brooksie spending the summer in Paris. Dad has said to me more than once, "Billy, we live in a world that is run by men who are run by women. You will be more content in life if you understand that"

Dad nailed that one. I know that, if I'm smart, I'll make peace with Brooksie and wish her Bon Voyage next month. If she falls in love with some sissy-ass Frenchman, we'll always have Oxford. And I'll still have my fastball. Besides, she has told me she loves me hundreds of times. I guess it is time that I start to believe her.

I'm going down the hall now and give her a call. It's time to write the next chapter of the *Nancy and Billy Love Story*.

May 10, 1964

Today started with Pauly Biadasz sticking his ass in our door at the crack of dawn (pun intended) and farting Reveille perfectly in tune, while screaming "get your young asses up boys, we be graduating in four weeks. *Love and honor* baby... *Old Miami, New Miami* baby (quoting from the alma mater). Then you can kiss Oxford a big fucking goodbye."

That will get your immediate attention on a couple of fronts. No rest for the wicket with Badass around.

Well, I must say that baseball provided the best distraction to my own personal French Revolution. Mid-week, while I was resting my prize-winning right arm, we beat the holy shit out of Xavier on Tuesday, then skinned the Cincinnati Bearcats on Wednesday. It didn't strike me until we were going through warm-ups at UC Wednesday afternoon, but somehow, we played both of our games against the Cats this year in Cincinnati. It is usually a home and away deal.

And we never play UC in football at home. Every year it's at Nippert Stadium. Doesn't seem fair. But the important thing is that we won both games easily, including my one and only perfect game last month.

The big deal came over the weekend with Kent State at home. I finally got back to the mound on Friday and pitched a two-hit shutout. My fastball was on fire. I turned Len Billet's catcher's mitt into the face of Charles De Gaulle, or Maurice Chevalier or Louis Jourdan and tried to kill those bastards. I did make the mistake in the fifth inning, of giving Brigit Bardot's kisser a try. But half way through my windup her face turned into Brooksie's face, and that turned into a wild pitch that scared the crap out of the batter.

But, thanks to my ability to turn Kent into the French Foreign Legion, we won easily, by a score of 7-0. Our senior second baseman, Mike Lindsay had a huge day, going four for four with two round-trippers. Mike has started at second base since our first game of our sophomore year. And, these were his first two homers. He only stands five foot ten inches and pretty much disappears if he turns sideways. But Friday he must have had an extra helping of Wheaties. He went from spray hitter to slugger.

Unfortunately, Kent State had saved their ace for the game on Saturday. Frank Schiele is a huge human. We heard the Kent players refer to him several times as *Bunyan*, as in *Paul Bunyan*. And, the only thing missing is the beard. He isn't much of a pro-ball prospect, because all he throws are fastballs. But on Saturday that was all he needed.

Len Billet who is hitting over .400 at the moment, had two of our three hits, one his eighth homer of the season and we lost 3-1. This means we are now in a three-way tie with Kent and Ohio University for the lead in the Mid-America Conference, each team having one loss.

We have our work cut out for us, as we have last year's MAC champs, Western Michigan at home next weekend, and we end the season at Ohio U. Andy has advised me that I will be pitching the Saturday games in both of those series.

On a different front, a passel of big-league scouts are in the stands every time I take the mound. And I talk every day to Mom and Dad who report that the phone is ringing off the hook. Some teams are starting to float some crazy numbers trying to hook a big fish with some very big bait. Dad has recently retained Michael Goldman, another golfing buddy and prominent Cincinnati attorney, to help advise us through the process.

But my main problem is that my mind remains on Brooksie, Paris and trying to figure out what our future might look like in September.I am smart enough to know that my only option is to support Brooksie's decision to head off to gay Paree. So, I have listened and learned.

She and Jan-Mar will be bunking in a second-floor apartment on Rue Lepic just steps from the subway station, or the Metro, as it is called in Paris. This is a big deal, because it is near the famous Moulin Rouge and a short walk from where Vincent Van Gogh once lived. Well, cut off my fucking ear and hand me a paint brush will you please?

They are planning side trips to Zurich, Munich, Nice and Venice, with a five day stop in London on the way home.

At any rate, we now know all about Nan's summer, while I don't yet have a clue where I will be. Dad has told me that several of the teams have suggested that they wish to start me in double-A ball, which means I will be visiting the bigger hick towns. So, the Yankees would equal Columbus, Ohio, Minnesota means Charlotte, NC, Kansas City parks their AA team in Birmingham, Pittsburgh in Asheville, the Cardinals in Tulsa and my beloved Reds would hone my skills in Macon, Georgia. Notice a pattern? There's a good chance I'm headed south.

Many of the southern options play their games in what they call the Sally League, which is the baseball way of saying South Atlantic League.

In the mean-time across the street at Western College for Women they will be holding training sessions in early June for college kids who have volunteered to go into the deep south to register Negro voters. That makes my potential work in the South seem pretty insignificant. Even more interesting is that LT is thinking about signing up for that gig. To me it sounds like a suicide mission. But my buddy seems completely unfazed by the danger involved.

When you stop to think about it, my silly-ass problems don't mean shit. As Dad has told me several times lately, "Billy, when you start thinking you have problems, I suggest that you remember why your mother and sister went to Washington last summer."

Dad always keeps me grounded with his gems of wisdom. Last week he said to me, "Son, a fastball is just something for sale, but character can't be bought."

Mom, who loves to quote Henri David Thoreau, would put it this way, "Many men go fishing all their lives without knowing that it is not the fish they are after."

Amen to that. With two weeks left in the season we are right where we want to be. If we can run the table, we will be in the play-offs with a chance to go to the College World Series in June. Fingers crossed.

May 17, 1964

{{

W ow! What a week. We easily handled Dayton on Wednesday. Then on Friday we dodged a bullet. Bobby Conn started the game against a very good Western Michigan team and pitched seven shut out innings. However, we also failed to cross the plate after seven.

When Bobby lost his control, walking the first two batters in the eighth inning, Andy brought on Spike Chandler to put out the fire. Spike proved to be a great fireman. With the score still tied in the twelfth inning, Andy pinch hit for Spike to no avail, and replaced him with Chad Schmidt.

Chad did his job for three innings. At that point both teams were running out of gas, not to mention daylight. After Chad walked the first batter, Andy knowing a loss would be disastrous, did something he had never done and brought me in to relieve. Feeling my oats and unexpected adrenalin, I quickly retired three batters with a series of eleven fastballs.

With Western Michigan into their fourth pitcher of the game, Wally Pittman led off the sixteenth inning with a single to rightfield. Then Freddie Cohen lined one to right center advancing Wally to third.

Now, who am I to challenge another man's thinking? But why they would pitch to our best hitter is beyond me, but they did. And if you are expecting to hear about Len Billet's towering homer to win, forget about it. Instead, Len laid down the most perfect squeeze bunt you will ever see. With that, Friday night dinner turned into a celebration.

Better yet, I threw a one-hit shutout yesterday. Len hit number nine and number ten, one that took two bounces before it rebounded off of Withrow Court, and the other landed on the sixth green of the golf course, some 400+ feet away.

The only pain of taking two from Western Michigan, was that I let a no-hitter get away that would have tied the record for most ever by a college pitcher. To his credit, Len took the blame for calling for a knuckle ball with two strikes on their number eight batter in the eighth inning. My pitch failed to knuckle, and I heard the ball whiz past my right ear as it streaked into centerfield. But, Lenny Boy, it's not on you. Given the situation I should have shaken off Len's signal and gone with the heat. I was pissed for a half a second. Just enough to strike out their pinch hitter on three fast balls. But what the hell, we took two from last year's champs

My new nickname on the ball team is "Bonus Baby". And I have learned that there are some real consequences to big bonuses. The major leagues have something called "The Bonus Rule" which could require the team paying a large signing bonus to assign a kid immediately to their major league roster, and keep him there for two years. But since 1957 teams have found ways around this.

This is why Dad has engaged Mr. Goldman. We all agree that I'm not ready for Yankee Stadium.

Dad has said that Goldman is appropriately named, as he is worth his weight in gold. Goldman and my parents have signed a simple deal that will reward the attorney with five percent of my signing bonus. Period! End of story!

After the happy ending on Miami Field yesterday, Brooksie met me on the way into our locker room and whispered in my ear that all bets were off, and LT, Jan-Mar, Brooksie and I would be spending the night at the Eaton Manor Inn in beautiful Hamilton Ohio. I had been waiting to hear such a proposal for almost two months. I thought it was awfully French of her.

And pitching one-hitters makes a guy hungry for more than sex. The Eaton Manor is the closest thing Hamilton has to fine dining. But they don't have snails and they don't set anything on fire.

Mom, Dad, Mir and her Einstein boyfriend were all at the game yesterday, but they had to skedaddle right back to Cincinnati because it was Prom Night at good old Woodward High. As always, it was being held at Castle Farms Night Club in Roselawn, only a few blocks from our two-story abode on Corvallis Avenue. As with my prom four years earlier, the Cliff Lash Orchestra was providing the dance music. That brought back some memories.

Now I don't want to be indelicate about this, but the celibacy decision Brooksie and I made at the start of the baseball season may not have been the wisest. Last night we reconnected in a way that was both passionate and tender. As Dad told me long ago, when we had *The Talk*, there is sex and there is sex with love. Once you've experienced the latter you won't think much about the former. I think good old Dad nailed that one. Though you do hear many stories to the contrary.

This morning we all stopped at Frisch's (the scene of the crime) for breakfast. After that it was back to campus where there were several messages for me at the Swing Hall front desk. One was from Joe

Nuxhall, congratulating me on my season to date. Another was from my old buddy, Cincinnati Post sportswriter, Earl Lawson, keeping his promise to get back to me. I thought about tossing the Lawson message in the trash, then I had second thoughts.

After talking to Dad and receiving some sage advise about award-winning sportswriters, we agreed I should call him later today. The truth is that we have final exams coming up in two weeks and I need to hit the books.

So, I trotted down the hall and called Lawson. He surprised me when he very kindly congratulated me on the season to date. Then he advised me that he had learned that I was keeping a journal and thought it might be a great idea if he and I turned it into a book.

First, I was pissed, wondering how in the hell he could possibly know about the journal. Then I wondered who in the hell would want to read a book about a college athlete from Roselawn. Lawson had plenty of answers to the last question and none to the first. I told him I would have to give the proposal some thought. He said he would be happy to discuss this with my parents if I wished, once again proving he knew a great deal about me. We agreed to revisit this after we had dealt with the issue of Ohio University.

It struck me that I should take a couple of hours and read the ramblings I have recorded in this little journal of mine. So, I did just that over the past two days and holy shit, what a journey I've been on. If Brooksie saw this, she might never come back from France. If Bags saw this, he'd put a contract out on me. But who gives a shit about a middle aged rich white guy who sneezes silver dollars. And I've been pretty hard on Our Miss Brooks, or Queenie, as I now call her. Her only fault is having an IQ about 80 points lower than her daughter. But on the other hand, I think I have pretty well captured the essence of my senior year here at good old MU. And I also realize that Brooksie has contributed mightily to my success in the classroom. She is brilliant and I have tried my damnedest to keep pace. Nan took advance placement work at Our Lady of the Thoroughbred School for Outrageously Rich Southern Belles. Thus, while she is two years younger than me, she is only one year behind me at Miami.

Plus, I am also trying to keep up with my splendid sister Liz who can't sleep if she gets a B, which she has only done twice in her two years at Miami. Speaking of Liz, I am so proud of her. She hesitated to try out for the cheerleading squad. But my old girlfriend, Toni, reminded her that she can do back flips and so, fucking sis-boom bah Sis. She admits now that it has been fun.

And speaking of sisters, I just learned that Mir will be speaking at the Woodward graduation four days after I graduate from Miami. She is the official Salutatorian of her class. Yep, this has been a special year for the Boyd clan.

There are a few other problems with sharing my journal with Lawson. There is a lot of dicey language. And more importantly, it has a great deal of compromising information on a whole lot of teammates and friends... especially, LT and Jan-Mar. And I suspect Bo and Andy might want to kill me as well.

I don't really have time to edit the whole thing right now. I have to get through exams and make sure we handle Ohio U this coming weekend, so we can go to the playoffs. Concentrate Billy.

May 18, 1964

As I said, I did take time to read my journal start to finish. It took a good bit of time. Here is a big part of what struck me.I have been talking so much about me that I have ignored my family.

Being a part of a family where your parents get up every day, happily get dressed and go to jobs they love, is such a special example.

Dad, started working at Henkie's Pharmacy on Woodburn Avenue in Walnut Hills, at the age of 12. He learned to make sundaes, soda's, phosphates, and to split a banana, behind the Tennessee marble counter that was the Henke Soda Fountain, waiting on high school kids and learning while he worked. He learned how to work the big cash register and calculate sales tax. And he watched Charlie Henke make drugs to fill prescriptions. And most importantly, he learned from Mr. Henke, ethics and morals and how to treat people with respect and politeness.

Because of all of this, after graduating from Withrow High School,

Dad entered the University of Cincinnati School of Pharmacy in 1933 and went to work for Dow Drugs when he graduated in 1937. Two years later, wanting to be his own boss, like Charlie Henke, Dad signed a lease in a new little strip center at the corner of Section and Reading Roads in Roselawn, and Boyd Pharmacy was born. He also swooped up his new love from his college days, Kayleigh Broderick and made her Kayleigh Boyd. After a weekend honeymoon in Columbus Ohio, at the Neil House Hotel, and a dinner at Marzetti's, Mom and Dad rented a little apartment two blocks from Boyd Drugs, in Roselawn.

Mom, started her career as an English teacher at Walnut Hills High School, while Dad got busy making pills. Unfortunately, a little Nazi with a stupid little mustache was busy with something also in 1939.

By the time I was born in July of 1942, Dad had started Officer Candidate School at Camp Picket in Virginia and was soon tending wounds as a Second Lieutenant and Medic at El Alamein, in Northern Africa. In the meantime, Mom had quit her teaching job at Walnut Hills High School in order to help run Dad's drug store while two young pharmacists were taking care of the drugs. As they are happy to admit, Mom and Dad drew up Liz during a quick furlough in mid 1943. They are also happy to fess up to the fact that the first thing they did when Dad returned from the war was rush down the hall and create Mir.

By early mid-1946, we were a family of five, camping in our new two-story house on Corvallis Avenue, thanks to the GI Bill, which also helped to bolster Boyd Drugs. Mom was back in the classroom by that fall and my parents were living their dream and building dreams for their three young children.

All of my life, I have heard Dad try to explain how the Boyd Clan, which is mostly Scottish, is, in our case, both Irish Catholics and Protestants. Dad is definitely Irish, but not too damned Catholic. As he says, the nuns at St. Francis De Salles beat the Catholic out of him.

However, if you are looking for authentic Irishmen in our family, I present to you the Broderick side, from County Cork. My mom's father, Patrick "Paddy" Broderick, comes from the truly genuflecting side of the tribe. A third generation, rosary-gripping, confession-giving, Guinness-drinking cat was Gramps Paddy until my Jewish grandmother, Ruthie Shulman changed all of that.

Bottom line; the Roselawn Boyd family represents a healthy mix of Americana. As far as I'm concerned, Ozzie and Harriet Nelson have nothing over on us.

Just one last word about Mom. Liz, Mir and I have learned more from her than you'll ever find in college. She has an intellect, a wit and a capacity to love like no one else I know. If my feet are on the ground, it is because of her. If all of that is a little too thick, so be it. My mother and father are special, and I should have made that point sooner. And never before in my life has that been more important than it is now.

OK, that's enough simple syrup from Billy Broderick Boyd. Back to the books and baseball. I might even run down to Sauer's Jewelry soon.

Tomorrow, we have Dayton at home and I'll be on the mound. But it comes down to the whole shebang this weekend at Ohio U, in Athens. MAC champs or not? College playoffs or not? What Big League team will want me the most? How much will they pay? Will Brooksie say yes? Or, is it still too soon to ask? Stay tuned.

May 20, 1964

W ell, I hope I didn't waste it all yesterday. I may have had my best stuff ever. Yes, the Baseball Gods were with me. Another perfect game and 20 strikeouts. I never would have admitted it, but breaking the record for most no-hitters by a college pitcher was important.

Everything was working. I might have pitched a *no-no* with just my fastball. But it was the three knuckleballs, five curve balls and eight sliders, all brilliantly called by Len Billet, that gave me the perfection. Happily, Len also got another dinger in the 5th inning.

The weather was perfect, as was the crowd. Mom, Dad and Liz were there. Bags and Queenie flew up in the Christmas plane. I must admit it meant a lot to me that they did. The baseball season has done much to humanize them in my eyes.

After the game, Brooksie was beaming. Following several interviews and signing a few autographs for the local Talawanda school kids, the Boyds, the Brooks along with LT and Jan-Mar moseyed over to the Rez and had dinner at the Zebra Room in side-by side booths.

At this point, Nan and Liz have become like sisters. It is very gratifying that after hurting Liz' best friend like I did, that she did not hold it against Brooksie.

LT provided Dad and me with the huge favor of chatting up Bags most of the evening, acting like he gave a rat's ass about horses and airplanes. Old Larry took it, hook, line and propeller.

Earl Lawson ran me down at the dorm last night from Cincinnati, where the Reds had lost an afternoon game to Milwaukee. 4-2. As always, Lawson was polite, very complimentary, with just a subtle reminder that my journal, with a few *Earl refinements*, could make a really nice book for a minor league pitcher (no rush, of course).

So, we are now down to it. We will jump on the chartered bus early Friday morning for the ride to Athens Ohio, where our destiny awaits. Mom, Dad and Mir, with Sidney Warren in tow, will drive over for the Saturday game. LT, hoping that Nellie Belle will hold up, is driving up Friday with Liz and Jan-Mar up front and Squeaky and Badass in the back seat. Squeaky and Badass will be bunking at the Phi Delt House, Liz with her old Woodward friend Sally Worthmann at the Pi Phi House and LT and Jan-Mar at the Holiday Inn House, on the edge of Athens.

Bags, is planning on flying up to Oxford in his new wings early Saturday morning, where he will pick up Brooksie and the two of them should be in Athens well before gametime. Queenie is tied up with a Junior League event. Her loss. AAA could not have planned it better with a Trip-Tik.

Marco Bellini will try to keep the dream alive in Friday's game. With OU sending six lefties to the plate, it had to be our southpaw on the mound. A little nervous? No shit. But a lot more excited. Let's do it skins!!

May 21, 1964

D ad drove up to campus this afternoon. After my perfect performance on Tuesday, he has been inundated with phone calls
including several offers. I guess the Yankees are sensing the pressure,
and have also finally floated a number. They are offering $85,000 for
signing with them.

As it turns out that is not the largest number being proposed. But,
as part of their deal they will pay an additional $50,000 when and
if they bring me up to the world-famous New York Yankees. Mom
and Dad both like the offer, in part, because I would be playing in
Columbus, a short two hour drive up the new Interstate 71 from
Cincinnati.

On the other hand, it is hard not to get emotional about the Reds.
They are offering $95,000 and want to start me in AAA rather than
AA. This means I would be assigned to their San Diego Padres farm
team. Dad spoke directly with Bill DeWitt, the General Manager of

the Reds, who pointed out a significant advantage with them is that I would be playing for a guy named Dave Bristol, a young fireball, who has been very successful in San Diego. What DeWitt didn't point out is that San Diego is a long 40-hour drive from Cincinnati, so no one will likely be driving out to watch me pitch. For some reason, Indianapolis is in the Pacific Coast League, so I would be within striking distance twice this season. The bigger question is would I be better served in AA or AAA?

Then there are offers from Kansas City, the Chicago White Sox and the Sox of a different color in Boston. I could tell that dad's head was spinning. He was very insistent that we just let the whole matter stew until the season was officially over. So, our strategy is to act polite and disinterested. Thus, I officially don't give a shit. But I do hear that San Diego is quite nice.

Brooksie and I had an early dinner with Dad at Mac and Joe's uptown. Nan and my father really like each other, which is a very good thing. And I hear that Mac likes Joe. I'll say this, they make a good burger.

Tomorrow, we head to Athens Ohio and a date with Ohio University. What the fuck is a Bobcat anyway? And Cincinnati, what the hell is a Bearcat? Who knows? But my dad is a cool cat!

Part II

There is no remedy to love but to love more
Henry David Thoreau

March 17, 2023

{{{

M atthew Boyd slowly closed the old leather-bound journal, and carefully laid it on his dorm room desk at Bradley Hall at the Ohio State University, in Columbus Ohio. It had taken him most of the day to read through the diary from almost sixty years earlier. Some of the sections he had read over and over trying to grasp the words on the pages. These, he realized, were his grandfather's words. But the process had left Matt feeling totally confused and unfulfilled.

His grandfather, William Broderick Boyd, had passed away in February, at Sarasota Memorial Hospital near his home on Anna Maria Island, on Florida's central Gulf Coast. After several weeks of grieving the wonderful man he knew as Gramps Boyd, Matt's father, Jack Boyd, handed Matt the dog-eared old journal, saying, "Matty, find some alone time and read this. When you are finished, share it with your sister. The two of you will want to talk to Grams Boyd when you've finished."

Matt looked down at the faded leather book with the Miami University seal embossed on the cover. All he could whisper half out loud was, "What the hell? And on St. Patrick's Day, no less. Get me a Guinness"

After sitting at his desk for a while, staring out the window at the late winter snow, Matt picked up his grandfather's journal and read the last few pages once again.

When he had finished, he reached for his I-Phone and spoke into it, "Hey Siri, call Grandma Boyd."

After a few rings, Matt heard his grandmother pick up.

"Well hello Matty. How are you dealing with all of that snow up there?"

Not waiting for an answer, she continued, "So, your father has told me he has shared Gramps journal with you. I know you and Caitlin, will be headed down this way next weekend for Spring Break. What do you say we try to get together for dinner on St. Armand's Circle for a little chat?"

"Grams, I think we are going to need a little more time than that. Can we come to your place when we get in Saturday?'

"Of course, darling." She responded. "We will have a lot to talk about and I know I have a great deal to explain. Bring that little book with you."

Matt ended the call and immediately dialed his younger sister, Caitlin Boyd on the campus of Northwestern University in Evanston, Illinois. He spent the next hour summarizing their grandfather's journal, while trying to answer unanswerable questions from his sister. All Caitlin could say was, "That is unbelievable. It is good we are both going to see Grams next week. I sure didn't think we would be spending spring break discussing family history. And who the hell is Nancy Brooks?"

MARCH 23, 2023

As the Delta 737 touched down at the Sarasota International airport, Matt flicked his phone out of airplane mode. Since leaving the snow and grey behind in Columbus, he had been alone with his thoughts and his free tomato juice, anxious to connect with his grandmother and sister across the bay on Anna Marie Island.

He noted a text from Caitlin that stated her flight had been delayed in Chicago. It looked like she would be a few hours behind him.

Matt collected his checked bag, walked out of the Sarasota terminal into a bright and familiar Florida sunshine, looking for his Uber. Less than a minute later he was headed north on US 41. The ride took just over a half an hour, as the Lexus 350 Matt had booked, pulled up to 5200 Gulf Drive, on Holmes Beach, where his grandparents had maintained a beach front Condo for almost twenty years. It was a warm special place, not just because it sat on the Gulf of Mexico, but more importantly, it was where the sun had set on his marvelous grandparents since his grandfather had retired as head of the English Department at the Ohio State University in Columbus Ohio, seven years earlier.

As he thanked the Uber driver and collected his bags, Matt realized this was his first visit to this special place since before his grandfather had passed away. He was met at the door by his grandmother. Although she had recently turned seventy-nine, he couldn't help from smiling at how much younger she looked. His grandmother was still very pretty and in spectacular shape, thanks to years of tennis and golf. Matt couldn't tell you if Grams Boyd had gone to her prom at Miami some sixty years ago, but was sure, if she had, she would still fit comfortably into her prom dress.

"Hello darling," she said, reaching up to give Matt a big, warm hug. "It looks like your sister is going to be a little late. Whataya say we run down to the Ugly Grouper and grab some lunch?"

Matt had waited a week hoping to get some answers from Grandma Boyd. But he knew he would have to wait until Cailin appeared. So, he said, "Sure, Grams. Let's go get some fish."His Grandmother walked into the kitchen, grabbed the car keys from a hook on the wall and tossed them to Matt.

"You'll feel safer if you drive," she giggled.

Three hours later Caitlin had arrived and she, Matt and their grandmother took some iced tea out onto the expansive lanai, with a view of the Gulf, and sat down in a semi-circle. Matt pulled out the old beat-up journal setting it on the cocktail table and cut right to the chase, "Grams, who the hell is Nancy Brooks, and what the hell is all of this?"

With that Toni Boyd began to unlock the mystery of Billy Broderick Boyd for her two grandchildren.

Toni reached to the cocktail table and lifted up the old journal, paused, smiled at Caitlin and Matt, and began, "First, let me say that in May of 1964, Nancy Brooks was the love of Grandpa's young life. And then he lost her."

After taking a small sip of iced tea, she continued, "Let me pick up the story where it ends in Gramps' diary. It was supposed to be a huge weekend for him. The Miami baseball team eked out a close win over Ohio University on Friday afternoon. I am told that Saturday was a perfect spring day in Athens. Billy was on the mound hoping to help Miami win its first ever league championship in baseball. Everybody important in his life was there, with one exception."

Toni carried on the story, "At game time, Nancy and her father had yet to appear. Your grandfather was pitching almost flawlessly. By the start of the seventh inning, Miami was winning easily by a score of 7-0. Just before Miami came to bat, Bob Kurz, who was the Information Director for the Miami Athletic Department, located Kayleigh and Daniel Boyd in the stands and asked them to come with him. The news Kurz was to share was tragic and life changing."

Noting the look of angst on Caitlin's face, Toni reached out and squeezed her hand before returning to her story."

What Kurz was sharing with your great grandparents was that the flight containing Nancy and her father from Oxford had gone missing. At that point Kayleigh and Daniel made the decision not to share this with Billy. He finished the game, Miami won, and after being carried off the field by his teammates, Gramps found his mother standing with tears in her eyes."

Swallowing hard, Toni continued, "By the time the game had ended it had been confirmed that the plane had been found in Hawk Woods west of Athens. Nancy and her father were gone."

"With that, your grandfather started on a new and self-destructive journey. He somehow got himself to Huntington, hopped a train headed to Washington and did not reappear for almost two weeks. Miami quickly lost two games to Minnesota in the playoffs without knowing where Billy had gone."

"Eventually he ran out of money and called his best friend Lenny Trimble. Not only had he missed the playoff games, but he had missed exams, his graduation, Mir's high school graduation, and more importantly, Nancy's funeral. Lenny drove to Washington, picked up Billy and brought him home."

Caitlin asked, "are you saying he didn't graduate?"

Toni explained, "Well he did graduate from Miami. But not until much later. By mid-June, he was in Mississippi with Lenny, trying to register Black voters, and by September he was in infantry training with the Army at Ft. Benning in Georgia. He was still inconsolable, almost self-destructive. From what your Aunt Liz has told me he had taken responsibility for Nancy's death and was acting like the only one who could punish him sufficiently, was himself."

Matt asked his grandmother, "How come we have never heard any of this?"

"That is very simple, Matt. Your grandfather insisted that it was never discussed. He ultimately went to Viet Nam where he fought bravely, earning a Silver Star and a Purple Heart."

"I think the important thing in this story is that time does help to heal. He had finally found the will to live again while almost dying in Viet Nam, and came back with renewed purpose. By the time he finished with the Army in 1967, Len and Janet Marley were married and Len was the backfield coach at Miami. Your Aunt Liz was working at Proctor and Gamble and in a serious relationship with your Uncle Mike. Mir was starting her senior year at Northwestern and Grandma Ruthie had just passed away."

"But Gramps married you and became a college professor. How

the hell did that all come about?" Matt asked his grandmother. "Well, he was very lucky that Miami allowed him to test out in the courses that stood as incompletes from the second semester of his senior year. He finally graduated with the Miami class of 1968."

Toni Boyd continued, "Billy had developed a great curiosity about African-American history and literature during his time in the South in the summer of 1964. After visiting your Aunt Mir at Northwester, he applied and was accepted into the Masters' Program in their Department English with a focus on American Literature. By 1972 he had earned a PhD in Literature and published his first book, 'Writings from the South – A Gift to America' about Langston Hughes, Zora Neale, August Wilson and other African-American writers. With that, he was on a new path."

Toni took another long sip of tea and continued, "Before you ask, let me now answer the big question, how did your grandfather and I get together?"

She smiled at Caitlin and Matt and said, "If ever the word serendipity was appropriate, the spring of 1971 was it."

"After teaching high school art for four years in Columbus, I was accepted to the Chicago Art Institute Masters in Arts Program. I was living on a string in Old Town, working at a book store beneath my small apartment on Wells Street. I loved Chicago even though I was broke. I had started dating a very nice guy named Thomas McGill who was a young investment broker. It was a comfortable relationship totally lacking in any real passion."

Toni paused, gazing pensively out at the Gulf of Mexico. Matt and Caitlin exchanged glances as a smile began to creep onto their grandmother's face.

She turned back to them and said, "Then one Saturday as I was stocking some shelves in the fiction section, I looked up to see the magnificent face of Billy Boyd smiling back at me. Totally by accident, we had magically reconnected. I knew in that instant that I had never stopped loving that guy."

"We exchanged pleasantries and then he asked if we had the book 'The Autobiography of Miss Jane Pittman' by Ernest Gaines? The answer was yes. And that request turned into a 45-minute conversation and a date to have dinner that night at the Red Star Inn on Clark Street. From that point we were together every Saturday for the next year. Thomas McGill was out of my life, and I was in a totally unromantic relationship with my old boyfriend who was still morning the loss of the love of his life and finishing his PhD."

"And how did we get past all of that you might ask? Well, it wasn't easy. But I will tell you this, if you want to really develop a serious love it helps to start with friendship. And that is what happened over that first year. Billy and I became best friends. It was sorta like that movie, 'When Harry Met Sally.' It took a long time, but he was finally able to talk to me about Nancy Brooks. And that was something he had not done with anyone else. And he somehow knew he had to share his deep hurt with me. Without that, our friendship could not have turned into love. Without that, you two would not be here today."

At that point, Toni looked at the clock at the far end of the Lanai, noting that it was after five-o'clock and informed her grandchildren, "Listen, I have made us a reservation at Café L'Europe on the Circle. Let's get cleaned up and we can continue this at the restaurant. You'll get more out of me after a Cosmo or two," she joked.

Matt drove the three of them down to St. Armand Circle in his grandmother's white Audi A5, using valet to park. By 7:35 they were seated at their grandmother's favorite table where she was engaged in conversation with the Maitre d', Tony DeMilio.

After ordering drinks, Toni addressed Matt and Caitlin, "Well you two will be graduating soon. Matty, I know you have loved Ohio State Law School. And Caitlin, I hope you know how thrilled Gramps was when you chose to study at the Medill School of Journalism at Northwestern. So, what is next for you two?"

Matt laughed and said, "Grams, the journal please. You and Gramps were best friends. That's great. But can you please fill in some blanks and explain why we know so little about all of this?"

"Of course, darling. Let's see, where was I?"

"Friendship turned to love," Caitlin snapped as their drinks arrived.

Toni Boyd raised her Cosmo and said, "Of course. How did I finally snare your grandfather? Well, sláinte you two."

Knowing full well that Grams Toni expected them to respond as their grandfather would have, they simultaneously said, "l'chaim."

It was a Boyd thing.

Matt swirled his new favorite drink, an Old Fashion, around the single huge piece of ice in the fancy rocks glass and said to his grandmother, "Ok, I understand why Gramps never wanted to discuss a girlfriend that was tragically killed in a plane crash. But why would he hide the fact that for two years he was the best pitcher in college baseball?"

"Well in simple terms, Matty, he blamed not only himself, but baseball for her death. Without the weekend series with Ohio University, Nancy would never have been in her father's small plane. As I said, I became the only person with whom he would discuss this. And I learned that he just couldn't escape the fact that it was Nancy's love for him and her desire to support his incredible baseball journey, that had put her in that plane."

Looking at Caitlin Toni Boyd continued, "I can tell you this. It was just too painful. Those of us who loved him, learned to just leave it be. It was his mother, Kayleigh that made that clear to us all. We just needed to let him bury baseball along with Nancy."

After pausing for a sip of her Cosmopolitan, she said, "The fact that every once in a while, though it was rare, your grandfather found he could purge some of the demons by reaching out to me. We would have very short talks. Well, not talks really. Mostly I would listen while the pain and guilt poured out of him. There was no better evidence of how much he came to love me. And every time this would happen, it ended with him taking me in his arms and holding me tight."

"That seems so sad," Caitlin said.

"I suppose it does sound sad. But truthfully, it was liberating for us both. The fact that his friends and family learned to respect his need to bury the first half of 1964 was incredibly important to his eventual healing. Thankfully, he gave me his journal when we were first married along with his permission to share it after he was gone. He didn't want to hide it. He just couldn't deal with the story it told."

"And try to remember, his experience in the south that summer and especially his time in Viet Nam changed him also."

"No sooner had Gramps arrive in Viet Nam, that he found himself in the middle of the Battle of Xa Cam My, where his unit was ambushed by the Viet Cong. They lost 36 men. Over the next six months, he was constantly under attack. And this wasn't a place where you could walk down the hall, brush our teeth, take a shower and climb into bed. The bottom line is that your grandfather endured ten months of hell. Then on January 8, 1966, in something called Operation Crimp, Gramps was wounded while clearing tunnels, when a soldier nearby stepped on land mine. Billy's wound was superficial and he stayed with his unit after being patched up."

Toni gave her grandkids a chance to let that sink in then went on, "Your grandfather came back from Viet Nam wounded... not so much physically, but more emotionally. He once said to me, 'I used to think that to encourage a teammate that struck out or made and error as a big deal. But when you see a guy with whom you had just shared some C-Rations get blown up and leave the world forever, right before your eyes; Well after that you feel a real responsibility to put your own life to good use.' The unspeakable carnage he witnessed in Viet Nam could never be washed away. But, as I said, it had served to give him new purpose."

The waiter showed up at this point, and Toni gestured at her nearly empty cocktail glass, indicating she wanted another Cosmo. In contrast, Caitlin and Matt had hardly touched their drinks.

She smiled again at the two youngsters and resumed the story.

"As you now know, he had lost the love of his life. He had walked away from certain fame and fortune never to give a career in baseball a further thought. And then there was Viet Nam. He has always said to me that he didn't want to be rich, he didn't want to be famous. He just wanted to do good and contribute in some way that would honor those people in his life that he had lost. That is why he chose to become a college professor. It is why he chose literature. And, ultimately, I think, it is why he chose to share his life with me."

"I have never resented the love he had for Nancy Brooks. She was a very special young lady. I had learned this from your Aunt Liz. I never worried if your grandfather had loved Nancy Brooks more than he loved me. I no longer believe that he did. His love for her was all that young love is supposed to be. I just needed to know that he could move on. Ultimately, we found a love much more special than I could have ever expected."

After the waiter placed a fresh Cosmo in front of Toni, she continued, "After accepting a teaching job at Northwestern in 1973, your grandfather asked me to marry him on Christmas Eve. I wanted to scream YES! But in order for us to happily move on, I took a huge risk. I insisted that your grandfather and I visit Nancy's grave site at the Lexington Cemetery, during a visit back to Cincinnati, before I could accept his proposal of marriage. He had never been there. Not even for her funeral. And he was not pleased with me. But he understood and finally agreed."

The waiter approached their table, but Toni waived him away and went on, "The Brooks family had a beautiful family plot next to a pond that was surrounded by four weeping cherry trees, two delicate white dogwoods, and a single low-cut lilac bush. At the foot of Nancy's grave her mother had planted Lillie-of-the-valley in a small planter. It was quite solemn, but beautiful, in the spring of 1974, when we visited."

"While we stood over that grave, I was the one who shed the tears. I simply said to Billy that I would never expect him to stop loving Nancy. I only needed him to love me enough to make a marriage from which we could build a life, a passion, a bond. When he took me in his arms that day, at that spot, and held me tight, I knew that I had the answer I needed. In the Jewish tradition, he picked up a small stone and laid it atop her gravestone. He never returned to the Lexington Cemetery again."

Toni reached across the table taking the hand of each of her grandchildren and said, "Matthew, Caitlin, I want you to fully understand that the life your grandfather and I had together was full of love, and yes, real passion, that no doubt was born, in part, out of the love he once had for Nancy Brooks. I loved that man the day I met him at Miami in 1962. And I was crushed when he walked away from me when he started up with Nancy. Frankly, I could not seem to find love after that."

"Everybody's lives were disrupted following the plane crash, including my own. And then, suddenly, he accidently walked back into my life and we both started to heal thanks to our friendship."

Caitlin asked, "Grandma, do you know what happened to Nancy's mother?"

"Well, we learned that Francis Brooks had sold the horse farm in Lexington in quick fashion and moved to Los Angeles. In 1970 she married the famous movie producer, Antoine Boucher, and spent the rest of her life with him in Beverley Hills and Paris. Once Billy located her, with my blessing, he sent Francis Brooks a dozen red roses on May 23, the anniversary of the crash, every year until she passed away in 1984. And they were always sent anonymously."

At that point, Toni said to Matt and Caitlin, "OK, let's take a little break and order dinner. Then you can ask me any other questions you may have."

With that she raised her delicate arm and the waiter hurried to their table like an obedient dog.

Matt picked up his menu and immediately noticed Escargot, Caviar and Caesar Salad and burst out laughing, remembering his grandfather's description of the Cincinnati restaurant, the Maisonnati, in the 60-year-old journal. After explaining his reaction, they all had a good giggle and proceeded with their order.

To honor the joke, they each decided to start with a Caesar Salad. Toni ordered her favorite, Atlantic Salmon with a Brandied Berry Compote. Caitlin decided to try the Snapper Margarita, and Matt ordered the Marinaded Veal Chop. His sister scolded him for ordering veal. So, Matt asked her if she knew how old the snapper was, while Toni delighted in the good-natured repartee.

As the waiter headed to the kitchen with their order, Toni said, "I know this is all a lot to process. And you both might feel a bit disappointed with your grandfather and me for carrying all of these secrets for so long. I would ask you not to dwell on the secrets, but rather try to understand how it all contributed to making Gramps the special person he was. For the rest of the night let's enjoy our dinner and time together and we can talk further about this tomorrow."

With that, Billy Boyd, and all of his skeletons in the proverbial closet, were set aside, and the conversation turned from the past to the future. That is until, Matt insisted they honor Billy one more time, by ordering Bananas Foster for the table.

"Good idea," laughed Toni. "Let's light this place up!"

March 24, 2023

T oni Boyd, as always was up at the crack of dawn and out the door for her morning walk, before 7:00. When she returned over an hour later, she found Caitlin on the lanai with a cup of coffee and her nose deep into her grandfather's journal. Caitlin reported that Matt had gone for a run on the beach. After pouring herself a cup of coffee, Toni joined Caitlin on the Lanai.

Caitlin said to her grandmother, raising Billy Boyd's journal, "You know Grams, this could be a book. With a little creativity, I think I could turn this into a fun and interesting novel."

That one caught Toni completely by surprise. To allow her brain to catch up with her emotions, she took a long sip of coffee and finally said, "Well, dear, I don't think Grampa kept that journal all of these years with the thought of somebody writing a book about him. And writing a novel is not an easy task"

Caitlin responded, "No, no. Not a book specifically about Gramps.

I'm thinking that it could be the basis of a novel... you know... fiction. All new names. And even a somewhat new story. But you have to admit that it is more than a little fascinating. And how you and Gramps reconnected is equally interesting. Of course, I wouldn't consider it without the blessings from you, and, for that matter, anyone else in here that is still alive. That would certainly include Uncle Len and Aunt Janet, and of course Aunt Liz and Aunt Mir."

Toni Boyd continued to process her granddaughter's suggestion. She finally said, "Well, I don't know. Perhaps you should start by talking to Matty and your father to see what they think. It is just something that never entered my mind. It is so personal and happened so long ago."

"Well, Matt will be back any minute. Can we discuss it with him?"

"Certainly," said Toni.

When Matt finished his run, took a quick shower and joined his grandmother and sister on the lanai, Caitlin got right to the point. After trying to make her case, Matt responded, "No way Cat. The only person whose permission you really need is not here to give it."

Then, looking at his grandmother Matt said, "Grams, he kept this from his own family his whole life. Certainly, he wouldn't want someone to turn it into a book now that he's gone."

Toni smiled warmly at Matt and responded, "Matty, that was exactly my initial reaction to Caitlin as well. But truthfully, I don't think it was the story he was trying to hide. It was more the hurt and the pain that he was carrying. I guess if Cat can turn this into something happy and optimistic, which is exactly what your grandfather became, then I don't see the harm. She has spent four years at Northwestern learning to write and develop stories. I think I can trust her with this. But I do agree that she should discuss it with your father, LT, Jan, Liz and Mir."

"Well, if she does this, she needs to run the final draft by everybody, I think," said Matt.

Toni reacted immediately, "No Matt. It would be her project and we would have to put our full trust in Caitlin to tell the story in her own way. Frankly, the more I think about it, something like this from Cat would finally close the circle on this old story, and would honor not just your grandfather, but also Nancy Brooks."

Matt took a deep breath, smiled at his sister and said, 'Well, Cat, I guess you need to make some phone calls." Then he said, "What's for breakfast?"

Toni laid out a morning feast, that was attacked in typical Boyd fashion. After they had all cleaned up the kitchen, Matt went to his room to pack, as he was scheduled to hook up with several of his lawyer-want-to-be friends from Ohio State School of Law, on Sanibel Island, two and a half hours south, where he would spend the balance of his spring break.

Caitlin, on the other hand was making new plans. First, she went to Toni and asked if she could spend the week with her rather than going, as planned, to Clearwater Beach to connect with her friends from Northwestern. She knew she would still have to pay her twenty-five percent of the condo rental, but she was now on a mission.

Toni asked her if she was sure she wanted to spend her last spring break with a seventy-nine-year-old, then told Caitlin that she would love nothing better. The only plans Toni had for the week was her regular Tuesday evening bridge group and nine holes of golf early on Thursday morning.

That settled, Caitlin called her roommate, Michelle Franklin to break the news. One of the reasons Caitlin and Michelle had remained so close over the three years they had roomed together at Northwestern, was that Michelle was unflappable. Once Caitlin explained the recent developments, all Michelle had to say was, "Well, I'll just have to drink your share. If I wind up missing, check for me a Betty Ford's."

With the logistics out of the way, Caitlin dialed up her parents. Her mother, Stephanie Boyd answered. At Cailin's request, Stephanie put the phone on speaker, and quickly Caitlin was talking to both her mother and father. One of the first things Caitlin had learned in the study of journalism was how to guide the conversation in a favorable direction.

Thus, she addressed her father, "So Dad, Grandma, Matt and I have been discussing at length Grandpa's journal and they have both already agreed that it could be the basis for an interesting novel, and that it would be the perfect way for me to honor his memory. I will be getting to work on it immediately."

Caitlin heard her mother laugh before her father said, "Whoa there, Cat. That's a lot to digest. And I'm pretty sure your grandfather wouldn't approve. Plus, you need to finish out your senior year and settle on a job."

"Dad, I will guarantee straight A's for this last semester, and you know darn well that I will accept the offer from the Tribune."

Jack Boyd processed this, then asked, "Your grandmother approves of this?"

"Absolutely. She just thinks I should get a thumbs up from you, Aunt Liz, Aunt Mir and one of the stars of the story, Uncle Len. Plus, you need to understand that I am proposing a novel, not a biography. I can assure you that no one will recognize the characters. Grams has said she has complete confidence in me."

Stephanie piped in, "Come on Jack. You know we should both support Cat. If Mom is OK with this, then you should be also."

By the time they hung up, Jack Boyd almost felt like the whole thing had been his idea. His little girl had done it again. Her little finger had

Jack Boyd firmly tied around it, God love her.

In quick fashion, Caitlin had also obtained full, enthusiastic support from her two aunts. The minute her Aunt Liz heard that Toni, her old college roommate, was totally OK with it, she gave her approval.

Liz said to her niece, "I hope you know how special your grandmother is."

Caitlin assured her Aunt Liz that she never knew that more than she had in the last twenty-four hours.

After hanging up from her Aunt Mir, Caitlin sought out her grandmother to report her conversations.

Caitlin said, "Well Grams, that went well. For some reason I am dreading a call with Uncle Len. He is such a big part of the tale the journal tells. And I wonder how much of the story Aunt Janet really knows."

Toni said to Caitlin, "Darling, you have nothing to worry about with LT or Janet. You and Matt are both so lucky that your grandfather and I had friends like the two of them. They could not love you more if you were their own daughter. Frankly, the only stumbling block I worried about was your dad. I raised a pretty suborned Irishman. Thank God for Stephanie. Your mom keeps him in line. Now, go call LT, then we can have a drink on the Lanai and enjoy another glorious sunset."

If there was one thing Caitlin had learned from William and Toni Boyd was to practice the old adage, don't put off until tomorrow what you can do today.

So, she went back to the guest room and spoke into her phone, "Hey Siri, call Len Trimble."

After two rings, she heard her grandfather's lifelong friend sing into her ear, "Hey hot shot, how the hell are you and why are you bothering a decrepit old man like me?"

Caitlin laughed and said, "Well, it sounds like I have the right number. I guess you know why I'm calling, right? But actually, there is more to it."

She took a pause and then got down to business.

"I've been hanging out with Grandma Toni the last two days. And, I suppose you are aware that she has shared Grandpa's diary with Matty and me, from back in your days at Miami. So far today, I've spoken with Grams, Matt, Mom and Dad, as well as Aunt Liz and Aunt Mir, about an idea I have. I have suggested that maybe I could use that journal as the basis for a novel. But I have also promised to get your blessing before I proceed. I don't know if you ever saw the diary, but there is a lot of personal stuff in it about you and Aunt Janet. But I believe I can easily camouflage everybody's identity and tell a great story."

While Caitlin was taking a breath, Len Trimble laughed and said, "First, let me confess to something, and then make a very important point about my old buddy, B-3. My confession is that I would sneak peaks at that journal all of the time back in 1963 and 64. It fascinated me that your grandfather was not only keeping the damned thing, but, also, how religiously he recorded the goings-on of our lives that year. He left it sitting on his desk, and it beckoned to me. Secretly reading it, I learned a lot about myself."

Len continued, "Then after the plane crash, Billy disappeared for two weeks. While he was missing, I read the journal front to back a few times. The point that I believe is very important for you to understand is how unbelievably honest Billy was in detailing that year. I cannot recall a single misrepresentation of anything he wrote. I had always known how special my buddy was, even back in high school. What many might miss in just reading his little story is how modest he was also. Think about it, here was a guy that was on the cusp of signing the biggest bonus in the history of professional baseball. Then, life would crush him to the point that he chose to walk away from fame and fortune and never look back."

Caitlin listened intently. The more Lenny Trimble spoke, the more questions she had. For well over an hour, the famous LT opened up about, not just Billy Boyd, but all of 1963 and 1964, as well as what came after.

Caitlin grew up witnessing the special relationship between her grandparents with Len and Janet Trimble. Yet, she learned so much more in this singular conversation. And she could sense how therapeutic it was for the man she had always called, Uncle Len. For the first time the cat was out of the bag, so to speak. And new truths spewed between Len's I-Phone and Caitlin's.

Several things began to come into focus for Caitlin. Perhaps, first and foremost was how truly close a friendship her grandfather had forged with Lenny Trimble by the time Billy had started his journal in the fall of 1963. Equally obvious was how important that camaraderie was to both men up until William Boyd had passed away. Without LT, Billy may never have found his way back from the tragic death of Nancy Brooks or rekindled his affections for Grandma Toni.

And, as Len explained, without Billy Boyd, Len Trimble might never have married and spent a gloriously happy life with Janet Marley. Nor, would he likely have become a successful head coach at three prestigious universities and eventually, the Athletic Director at his alma mater. Lenny and Billy were clearly as close as any blood brothers might hope to be.

Len also filled in a lot of the blanks left by Caitlin's discussions with Toni, including how seriously broken Billy was after the tragic plane crash. He also explained the important role her great grandmother,

Kayleigh Boyd, had played in convincing friends and family to allow Billy to bury his baseball dreams along with Nancy. Billy just could not get past the fact that Nancy and her father were dead only because of a silly baseball game in Athens Ohio.

At one point, Len said to Caitlin, "Kiddo, the fabulous fastball throwing Billy Broderick Boyd, or B-3, that I had known, died in May of 1964 and he eventually came back as William Boyd, renowned English professor and author. It was when he started calling himself William Boyd that I started calling him Hopalong or Hoppy, because when we were kids there was a famous TV cowboy named Hopalong Cassidy and he was played by a handsome actor named William Boyd. But in my heart, Cat, he'll always be B-3."

Len continued, "At any rate, Kayleigh was as solid as a rock. She hated it when he joined the Army, and feared for his well being the whole time he was in Viet Nam. But she understood better than any of us, that he had to find his own way of healing. Thanks to her, we were all able to lay to rest the old Billy B-3 Boyd and embrace the new William Broderick Boyd. There were a whole bunch of life-lessons we learned from Kayleigh Boyd I can tell ya."

Caitlin heard Len say, "It's Caitlin. She's up to no good. Come here and get in on this."

After Janet and Caitlin said hello and exchanged pleasantries, Len continued, "I'll tell you one thing that Kayleigh understood, that the rest of us did not, is that fame is fleeting. Everybody insisted that you couldn't lay to rest Billy's fame by just refusing to talk about it or acknowledge it. But she was right. It eventually became less than a footnote. What B-3 had accomplished on the mound just evaporated by the time he came back from Viet Nam. And that was that. It wasn't discussed and was eventually forgotten. And as I told you, Billy became William and reinvented himself."

At this point Len and Caitlin explained to Janet the plans Caitlin was making to turn Billy Boyd's journal into a novel. Janet reacted by saying, "Well, I have to tell you Cat, that the story that has so many wonderful, happy memories, is still very painful for me. Nancy was very special to me. And, though I know better, I have never shaken the guilt I still carry about the plane crash. You see, I could have been on that plane. Nancy tried very hard to get me to fly with them to Athens. But I simply was afraid to fly with her father in that small plane. So, I drove to Athens with Big Daddy here. That weighs on me still."

"Wow," Caitlin said, while thinking to herself, this really is a remarkable story.

Len concluded the conversation by saying, "Caitlin, you know we love you. I will echo what your grandmother has said. We trust you to do this right, if you decide to go forward. So, feel free to talk to us as much as you need. And let's find a time soon to get together for a serious sit down to see how we can best help you."

"Thank you, Uncle Len. You too and Aunt Janet. I love you both. Let me get to work on this, and I will be in touch again soon."

Caitlin hit the red circle at the bottom of her phone, disconnecting the call, feeling a great sense of relief and an even greater sense of purpose. She walked out to the lanai where she found her grandmother reading the new Griffin Dunne book, "The Friday Afternoon Club" and sipping on a glass of Cabernet.

Toni reached out and squeezed Caitlin's hand, while nodding toward the developing sunset over the Gulf of Mexico and stated, "Look at that. How lucky am I to have something like that to gaze at most afternoons? Your Gramps and I started the habit of having late dinners because we would have drinks out here and watch the sun disappear on its way to Texas."

Caitlin held on to Toni's hand and said, "Well, you were right. I spoke with both Uncle Len and Aunt Janet. They could not have been more supportive. I've already learned a great deal and I am anxious to get started."Toni knowingly clutched Caitlin's hand a bit harder and asked, "Would you like something to drink dear?"

"No thanks, Grams. I think I'll just drink in the view."

NOVEMBER 23, 2023

Over the more than eight months since Billy Boyd's journal surfaced, life had changed significantly for Matt and Caitlin Boyd.

Matt had graduated from Ohio State School of Law. His Aunt Liz had long ago married attorney Mike Elam. A generation later, Matt's father, Jack Boyd, graduated from Georgetown Law School and joined his uncle's firm. Over the years, the firm had grown into one of Cincinnati's largest and most prestigious. Thus, in July, Matt became an associate at Fulton, Elam and Boyd Attorneys-at-Law, and was studying to take the Bar Exam in February.

Caitlin, after earning her degree in Journalism at Northwestern University, accepted a job at the *Chicago Tribune*. On the Newspaper's website was a profile of Caitlin which read:

Designation: Reporter

Author Bio: Caitlin Boyd is a reporter covering afternoons and evenings for the Metro desk focused on local government and goings-on throughout the north and northwest suburbs for the Tribune's *Pioneer Press*. She is a committed Chicago partisan and a native of Cincinnati, Ohio.

Gender: Female.

Caitlin loved her job at *The Trib* and living in downtown Chicago. In addition, she was using every spare moment on her novel with the working title, "A Love Story in Two Parts."

She had discovered that the writing was the easy part. The more difficult task was finding a publisher. You could not just send a transcript to Random House or Simon and Shuster and wait for the money to start rolling in. It quickly became apparent that she would need a literary agent. Her grandmother had put her in touch with her grandfather's old agent, Franklin Scott, in New York. However, Scott concentrated strictly on works of non-fiction. But he did refer her to two agents he strongly recommended in Chicago.

With the guidance of Senior Editor, Andrea McCauley, at the Tribune Metro Desk, who was in full support of Caitlin's attempt to become an author, Caitlin had recently engaged Literary Agent Steven Jackson. As it turned out Jackson's office was on West Huron Street just west of Michigan Avenue and six short blocks from Caitlin's office at the Tribune Tower. Things were now moving ahead nicely.

With Thanksgiving approaching, Caitlin had flown to Cincinnati on the Tuesday before Bird-Day. The Boyd clan were now all gathered at Jack and Stephanie Boyd's sprawling home in Mason, Ohio. It would be the first Thanksgiving without William Boyd handling the carving duties.

As everyone gathered around the two tables that Stephanie had set for the event, Jack Boyd said to his surrogate uncle, Len Trimble, "Uncle Len, would you honor Dad's memory by carving the turkey?"

Len stood up and replaced Jack standing over the huge roasted bird. Before picking up the electric carving knife, he raised his half-filled glass and said while choking back tears, "To my brother, Hopalong, Billy, B-3, and the best human I have ever known. Nobody could butcher a turkey like Hoppy, but I'll try."

Toni Boyd raised her glass and said, "Slainte!" Everybody else yelled in response, "l'chaim!!"

As Len went about the task of bird-butchering, it seemed that Chardonnay, Pinot Noir and tears were poured in equal amounts. As early generations of Boyds would have said, the whole teaghlach was there. From the oldest generation, was Len and Janet Trimble down from Oxford, as well as local Cincinnatians, Mike and Liz Elam, Bob and Mir Wilkens plus Toni Boyd, up from Florida. Cousins and third cousins to the hosts included three Elams and two Wilkins. And, of course, from the Gen Z, seated next to Jack and Stephanie Boyd sat their children Caitlin and Matt.

While feasting, the family traded lively conversation about their lives and current events until it was time for pumpkin pie and Stephanie's famous apple strudel, which was served along with coffee, tea and Jameson's.

Over desert, the conversation turned to Caitlin's book. The book had become a family project of sorts, as Caitlin had spent hours on the phone with every person around the two tables, building a more detailed profile of the characters from Billy's journal.

Of course, Toni, Len, Janet, Liz and Mir had proved to be invaluable sources, as Caitlin learned more and more about all of them and the magic that was the 1960s. She had reams of notes that were incredibly well organized. She was enjoying the journey of attempting to create an interesting work of fiction. Yet, there was a building pressure to not let down the people that now sat around her parent's Thanksgiving table.

The subject of Billy's baseball talents came up. Len Trimble offered something that stuck with Caitlin and helped to guide her to the finish line.

Len said to those gathered, "One of the things Billy said most often over the years was how lucky he was to have escaped the fame that would have come with baseball. He truly believed that nothing was more dangerous than fame. He was afraid that notoriety and wealth would have corrupted him. It really worried him."

Grandma Toni piped in, "That is absolutely true."

Cailin took her last bite of strudel, realizing she had just found her way to the end. She couldn't wait to get to her computer.

september 25, 2024

Toni knew it was headed her way and was thrilled when the UPS lady dropped a padded envelope at her front door. She carefully opened it and pulled out an inch and a half thick book entitled, "Gunner McCracken, a Love Story in Two Parts." Although Caitlin had told her it was almost 500 pages, Toni was surprised with both the thickness and the weight.

She immediately picked up her I-Phone and sent her granddaughter a short text, "Book has arrived. It is thicker than I had expected. Will start immediately and give you a call when I finish. Probably tomorrow." Then she added two heart emojis and hit "send."

It was one-thirty in the afternoon. After employing her Keurig to brew herself a Donut Shop coffee, she added some Half-and-Half and took her mug and the book out onto the lanai and settled into her lounge chair. She then spoke into her I-Phone and said, "Siri, play my soft classicals album."

She smiled as the strains of *Chopin's Nocturne in E-Flat Major* washed over her. She picked up the book, read the dedication, swallowed hard, choked back tears, then swallowed a big slurp of Donut Shop coffee, took a couple of deep breaths and went to the first chapter.

Over the next ten hours or so, Toni read and reread passages from Caitlin's novel, feeling more and more pride and wonderment with what her granddaughter had done with Billy Boyd's story. The characters were all there in full view, yet so cleverly disguised.

Around six in the evening she had moved to her den, switching from coffee to red wine. Just before midnight, a wide grin appeared on her face as she completed page 487, the last page. Toni was filled with such a mix of emotions... all good. The music had long ago ended. And she realized, in disbelief, that she had consumed almost a full bottle of cabernet. Toni closed her granddaughter's book with just a hint of a laugh and a single tear, once again reading the back cover from top to bottom.

> "First time novelist, Caitlin Boyd has crafted a brilliant sojourn back in time, to a magical place full of hilarious, yet very human characters. She captures the sixties as if she had lived through them herself. The journey is filled with twists and turns, as well as raw emotions. And while her main character, Gunner McCracken may seem both flawed and super-human at times, this book is exactly what the title implies. A love story in two parts."

New York Times: "Twenty pages in, I had to check the author's name, because I thought I was reading a book from the seventies by Dan Jenkins. But I soon knew better. And this is more than a Bildungsroman. Yes, in part, it is a coming-of-age story. But what Caitlin Boyd has ultimately crafted is a great love story."

Chicago Tribune: "This first novel by our staff writer, Caitlin Boyd, will have you rolling on the floor in laughter, before she rips out your heart. But not to worry, she will replace it with a new stronger and warmer one."

Columbus Dispatch: "It is true that Gunner Mc-Cracken never played quarterback for Ohio State. But Caitlin Boyd will have Buckeye fans wishing he had. What a page-turner with one fascinating surprise after another, some happy, some sad. And, yes, what a hopeful, optimistic story of true love."

Then Toni went to the front of the book to the Dedication Page and read these words:

"In memory of my Grandfather, William Broderick Boyd, who inspired me to write. And for my Grandmother Toni Jansen Boyd, our beacon in the darkness, who taught us how to live."

Toni reached for her phone and quickly typed a new text message to Caitlin that read, "Many tears, which is good. You really have honored your grandfather and also the memory of Nancy Brooks. It is OK that so few will know that. And, Cat, you have honored our family. So proud of you."

After sending the text message, Toni once again spoke into her phone, saying, "Hey Siri, play songs for Billy and Toni."

She was rewarded with strains of the Frank Sinatra hit from over sixty years ago, *The Second Time Around*. As she drank in the lyrics that had become so dear to her and Billy, she walked into the master bedroom and laid the book on the night stand by the side of the bed where her late husband had slept. She ran her fingers over the cover and softly murmured, "I think this belongs to you Billy."

About the Author

R andy Stertmeyer is the author of "The Chrome-Plated Years, Almost True Stories of Growing Up in a Magical Time." He is a native of Cincinnati Ohio with a Bachelor of Science Degree in Education from Miami University, Oxford, Ohio and a Master of Arts Degree in History from Xavier University, Cincinnati, Ohio.

Randy spent a long career with several executive positions in the building materials industry, including serving as President and CEO of Green River American Hardwood and SureLock Industries. After a short retirement he joined Communicators International, Inc, a advertising/marketing firm as their COO.

Randy has two children, two step-children and nine grandchildren. He currently resides in The Villages, Florida with his wife Peggy

www.ingramcontent.com/pod-product-compliance
Lightning Source LLC
Chambersburg PA
CBHW061615170626
46811CB00001B/435